BROTHEREN

Rouged

A novel by: **Semaje**

BROTHEREN
Rouged

A novel by: **Semaje**

Published by In CTRL Publishing & Company LLC

inctrlpublishing@gmail.com

This novel is a work of fiction. Any references to real people, events, establishments, or locales are intended only to give the fiction sense of reality and authenticity. Other names, characters, and incidents occurring in the work are either the product of the author's imagination or are used fictitiously, as are those fictionalized events and incidents that involve real persons. Any character that happen to share the same name of a person who is an acquaintance of the author, past or present, is purely coincidental and is in no way intended to be an actual account involving that person.

Library of Congress Cataloging-in-Publication Data:
ISBN- 978-1-7351482-0-5
        978-1-7351482-1-2 (ebook)

I dedicate this book to my family, who has always been at the forefront of my life. To my wife Senobia; my children: Jamia, Jaylan, and James Jr.; and my mother, Maggie McNeely, for always believing in my dreams and aspirations. I hope that I make you proud each day.

*Don't lose focus. It seems that in the rush of everyday
life and our dreams of stardom, we forget to live.
Oftentimes, we miss our blessings waiting on a blessing.*

— SemajE

CONTENTS

•••••••••●•••••••••

PART FOUR:
I'm My Own Man

PART FIVE:
Unchartered Territory

PART SIX:
One Year Later

THE PACK

Four best friends took their last bow as the crowd went wild. The flashing lights from all the cameras set the boys' motivation level at an all-time high. The teenagers won a college talent show on the campus of Southern University in Baton Rouge. Glittered two-piece navy suits outlined in gold sequin set the stage afire as they performed New Editions' "If It Isn't Love." Some bomb-ass choreography, lots of stage lights to set the uniforms off, and four guys who could sing better than the original artists let those college students have it. Now that's one hell of a combination. Never before had they felt the excitement of hearing yells and screams of the people left in a trance by their act. How could high school boys come on a college campus and tear that shit down? Well, they did.

With D.J. in the lead role and the others on backup, they were a mixture of the old Jackson 5 and New Edition. At first, scared to even enter the competition, these friends found out that night, live on the stage would spark a flame in them that would decide their paths for the rest of their lives.

That night the boys lay in the backyard of Kendall's house, camping out and looking out over the stars as they could smell the fresh air from the bayou not far away thinking about what life would be like for them in the future. The boys' sleeping bags lay in a circle around the trophy they won.

"Man, did you hear the crowd tonight?" D.J. said, "I don't think that I've ever been so excited and so scared in my entire life." "Yeah, that's because you are the only one who truly has the gift. I mean, we can all sing, but your voice is something totally different." Kendall said.

1

"Come on, man, it was not just me; we all did a great job," said D.J.

"You damn straight!" Trip said, "I know that the ladies were jocking me! Who has eyes as pretty as mine?" Trip blinked his deep green eyes. "Shut up, fool! You always think that someone is looking into your damn face, you ain't all that. You're not even old enough to worry about that, you Lil' pervert," Ped'east said obviously tired of Trip's bragging.

"Fuck you, stupid," Trip said, never holding his tongue.

"C'mon, fellas, we just won one of the biggest shows in Baton Rouge, and we could take this city," Kendall said.

"No, man, we have much more territory to take than that. We gotta get out of this God-forsaken town and take it all the way to the big time." D.J. yelled.

"Yeah, I feel ya, dude, let's do it." Ped'east agreed.

"What's bigger than Baton Rouge?" Trip said.

"Anything is bigger than here. Let us go to New York. I know that is a big-time!" said D.J.

"Hey, let's make a pact that no matter where college or life takes us, we will meet up in New York and make this fame thang work!" Kendall said.

The boys lay back on the sleeping bags really wondering if it could all be really possible. Hell, they were just boys and how many people really got out of Baton Rouge once you get locked in here. The furthest I think people go is Texas and that's only because Six Flags is there. Could they really get out?

"Hey, let's do like the white boys do and cut our fingers to make this thing official," D.J. smirked full of excitement.

"Are you stupid, man, I'm not cutting my finger to do no stupid shit like that, you trippin!"? Trip said.

Trip received his name from being Marcus Cummings, III, as in triple, and besides that, he was always getting on everyone's nerves. Everyone always said that he was tripping, and so "Trip" was the name that seemed to stick with him. Trip was younger than the other boys. Although he was a preteen, he still felt that he could hang out with his brother and his friends. Trip got on their nerves, but they all seemed to not mind him being around. He was their Lil' brother, even though they didn't have the same bloodline with him except D.J.

"Come on, Trip, I think that is a good idea," Kendall said. He jumped up and ran into the house, pull out a small knife from the kitchen drawer, and eased past his mother back to the solace of his "blood brothers" to be. Kendall was excited, as well as D.J., but Ped'east and Trip were not so happy about the idea. Reluctantly, they decided to go along with the rest of the guys. D.J. was the first to prick his right index finger, and then Kendall, followed by Ped'east and Trip. Making the oath, the boys put their index fingers together to symbolize their acceptance of the oath. "No matter what, this dream shall become a reality." D.J. said. "That sounds so stupid," Trip said, giggling to himself. In unison, the other boys said, "Shut up, Trip!" "And get some sleep, big head," the big brother said to Trip. "Fuck all, y'all," Trip grunted.

Even though the boys were joking around, they would never know the impact of that pact that they had just made would influence their lives. It would be the creed they governed themselves whenever they needed one another. The boys began to fade into a deep nod, one by one, all except for D.J. As he lay out looking up at the stars, his mind was clouded with notions of fame and fortune. He knew he had the talent to make in the Big Apple, but there was so much work to do to make his dreams come true.

Part One:

5 YEARS LATER

CHAPTER ONE

Wednesday morning found D.J. standing in the line getting ready to be fitted for his cap and gown. He was prepared to start his new life. During the fitting, tears began to form in his eyes. There had been so many memories that he would be leaving behind. D.J. quickly wiped his eyes before anyone could notice that a grown man was standing there about to cry. That was not the image that he wanted to leave for himself, but the thought of his life at school away from home were great memories he knew that he would cherish forever.

Morehouse was his home away from home. It had been the place where he became a man. To tell the truth, Atlanta was the place where you would either find yourself or lose yourself.

D.J. was determined to make a life for himself in the city. He tried his best to do that every day, but his time in the city of Atlanta was almost over. A-town was a place of culture, a place where hundreds of African-Americans traveled to be a part of its rich environment. It was the new Black Hollywood. In the daytime, the hustle and bustle of busy men and women filled the air with a new beginning, a diverse lifestyle of an accomplished atmosphere of those who had sought and found success. The nightlife was so different. You could almost reach out and touch the welcoming vibes of hip-hop, jazz, reggae, and classical, all balled up in one lump sum of adventure. You could taste the sultry slick passion of those who ran the night totally camouflaged by the darkness. "Hotlanta" was the Black man's heaven.

Academics were priority on D.J.'s list, but the greatest ambition was his hopes of becoming a major singer. Ever since that talent show years before in Baton Rouge, D.J. dreamed every night of being a singing sensation. He knew that with those aspirations, Atlanta was the place. His parents thought that he was responsible enough to take care of himself, but D.J. had doubts about their praise of him. His grades were excellent, but the thought of being on his own was frightening. The one thing that kept him focused was that nightly dream that always reminded him of his commitment to himself, being famous. Now, four years later, D.J. had been at the top of his game.

D.J. worked at a pizza place during the week, but on the weekends, he sang in *Jacob's Night of Life* nightclub. This is a place where all of his peers hung out. Singing was the only thing that really made him feel alive, like his life had a purpose. He tried to land gigs at the most high-class night clubs where the stars would frequent, but the timing was never right, or something always came up, but whatever the reason, he never got the opportunity to shine for the "big wigs." He was content with the club that he was in solely because he just wanted to sing. In college, he had taken several classes in music and had even written a couple of songs, that he never put them out there. He felt that he wasn't ready for that type of exposure, not just yet. There were plenty of disappointments, but he knew that in that business, there would be. He continued hoping for the best and his big moment.

He had been on interview after interview and had not landed a contract. He heard so many different excuses. "Hey son, you are good, but you don't have an angle." "I love your voice, but I don't have room for you on the label." "I'll get back with you. Stay by the phone." This was a cruel business, but he was determined to make it.

D.J. got back to his apartment at 8:00 p.m. All of his things were still unpacked. His parents were going to kill him. They had told him they would be there the next morning with a U-Haul to bring all of his things home, and he still had not packed anything.

Ring. Ring.

"Hello"

"What's up, nigga?

"Stop cursing man. You know that yo momma would kick yo ass if she heard you talking like that!"

"Whatever. I am at the airport. Why don't you come and pick a nigga up."

"What? What are you talking about?"

"Are you deaf? I said, come and pick a nigga up! Trip started to laugh in the background. He knew that his brother hated to hear him talk like that, and he did it to aggravate him.

"Why are you here?"

"What do you mean" Ain't you graduating Saturday morning?"

"Yeah, but that still does not tell me what you are doing here."

"Look, Mom and Pops are driving in on Friday night, and I did not want to take that long ass ride, so I convinced them to let me fly here today. You know that they are a little freaky and love the idea of riding together alone so that Pops can lay that pipe down." Trip knew that D.J. didn't like that either, but hell, it was so much fun to get his brother to blush.

"Boy, you better stop talking like that before I have to snatch yo skinny ass." D.J. smiled on the other line, even though he didn't like the way Trip was talking.

"That is a nasty visual, I don't want to hear that."

"Look, you coming or not?"

"Yeah, I'm coming."

"Hurry up, you know that the only reason that I came is that I wanted to stick this meat in some fortunate Atlanta broads." Trip laughed again. He knew that D.J. had heard enough.

"Hey, you stop talking like that. You know that I'm not too fond of it, and now you are going too far. You are only a junior in high school, and you should not be thinking about that."

"I know that you are kidding. You know that I am not still a virgin. I left that island years ago. I have not been a virgin since my freshman year. Come on, big brother, you know me. I am who I am!"

"You are stupid! I will be there in about twenty minutes. Bye." D.J. hung up the phone with mixed emotions. He had really been the one who helped his little brother to grow.

Trip had been into all kinds of mischief, and his parents were tired of him. Although D.J. was studious, Trip never brought home good grades. Everyone figured smarts ran in the family until Trip started bringing grades home. It didn't matter to D.J., though. He loved his little brother, and he was probably the only who could understand him. No one else could talk with him. Whenever their parents had enough, they would send in D.J. to reason with Trip. Every summer, D.J. saved his money to put his brother through summer school. His mother would always say, "I ain't paying for education in the summer when it is free all year long!" The father would agree, and D.J. would be left to take care of Trip's academic summer. But, of all of the madness that Trip got into, his one love was dancing. He was the best dancer there was, according to D.J. His brother had the magic feet, and people seemed to be mesmerized at his ability. Trip was more than a dancer; he was a natural performer. He won every talent show that he entered. His parents never thought that his dancing would amount to anything, so they blew it off and never gave him credit for the one that thing in his life that he was great at doing.

D.J. walked into the airport to face with a massive grin full of braces. His brother was such a warming welcome to him. Even though this boy was very immature, he loved him beyond belief. "Big brother, what's up, man?" Trip walked briskly toward his brother with hand extended. D.J. smiled as though he was being greeted by Ed McMahon with a ten-million-dollar check.

"What's up, little brother?" D.J. extended both arms as if to give his brother a big hug. "I know that you are not about to hug me."

"That is so gay. You know that I don't play that shit!"

"You are stupid. It is nothing wrong with greeting another man with a brotherly hug. And that word is not acceptable, so cut it out!"

"It is when you are standing in the airport with all of these strange ass people watching. You know that I don't like all of that mushy shit anyway. And I don't think that word is so bad." "Whateva, get your bag, and come on."

"Oh, a brotha comes this far to see you and you ain't gonna give a man a little special treatment and get a brotha's bag?"

"Nigga, I'm the one graduating. You are not special! You should have a gift for me. You better stop trippin!" Trip stopped smiling. "You must be on some crack! You know that my endz ain't tight yet, and I will have to hit you up some other time, playboy!"

"Do you always have to talk in slang? Do you know any standard languages?"

"Fuck no, Ese!" Ese was the only Spanish word that Trip knew, and he thought that was very funny. "Me not know no other languages." Trip said with a Hispanic accent.

D.J. knew that it was useless. He knew that he couldn't change his brother, so he just let him be. "Come on, man, let's go." They made it out to the car and headed toward D.J.'s apartment when his cell phone rang.

"Damn!" Trip said with a devilish grin, "Punanay is calling already?"

"You go, boy!" D.J. looked at Trip from the corner of his eye. It was going to be a long weekend.

"Hello"

"Hey, old man, I know who this is," D.J. said jovially. "Did your stupid ass brother make it there safely?" "Yes sir, we are on your way back to the apartment now." "What? I told his behind to call as soon as that plane touched down. I know his plane was scheduled to land almost an hour ago."

"Hold on, Take the phone, stupid, you know yo little behind is in trouble."

"Damn, that is daddy, huh?"

"Yep!" D.J. now had the devilish smile. Trip took the phone. From the look on Trip's face, his dad was letting him have it although he couldn't hear what they were saying.

"Okay, Dad, I'm sorry!" Trip handed the phone back to D.J.

"Dad, calm down, calm down. I have him, and I will make sure to take good care of him. You have my word. Tell mom that I love her and I can't wait to see her. I love you too, dad!"

"Hey, we love you too, son. We are so proud of you. Our Morehouse man! Hey, D.J., D.J.? Look, your mother and I are going to be a little late, but we will be there in time for graduation." D.J. chuckled slightly. He thought about the comment that Trip had made about his parents.

"Hey, what's so funny, son?"

"Nothing, dad. That is fine as long as you are there when I receive my degree."

"You know that we would not miss that for the world."

"Alright, old man, see you Saturday."

D.J. hung up the phone and began to speak with Trip about his behavior. "Trip, you have got to be more responsible, man. You know that is the biggest thing that they always have to say about you."

"Come on, D, not the lecture, not today, please!"

"Hey man, I am not trying to come down on you, but I want you to understand that you are not a little boy anymore. You have to start taking care of your business. You had many times in your life that you could have done the right thing, and you chose not to, but you do know right from wrong."

"Don't sit over there and act like you have not done any dirt. I am not in the mood for a lecture, okay? I came here to spend time with my big brother, not my father. If I want to listen to that shit, I would have come with yo parents."

D.J. paused for a moment. As he thought about it, Trip was right. It was not the time. This was going to be the best weekend of his life, and he didn't want to spoil it fussing about something that his parents were already giving to do. "You are right man, let's get something to eat and head back to the apartment."

"Wait, no females? I know that you have some plans to get with some broads, don't you?"

"Shut up, boy! Is that all you think about?"

"You are not gay, or you? I can handle the truth."

"Forget you, dummy! I ain't no punk, and I get mine, but that ain't something that I am about to share with your Lil' young ass! Are you hungry or not?"

"Yeah, let's eat."

D.J. knew that he had a character on his hands, but he wouldn't trade him for the world.

D.J. never imagined the emotion that the graduation ceremony would bring him. As the band leads the graduating class into the stadium, the memories of his time in ATL flooded his mind. Atlanta allowed him to seize a wealth of knowledge, both academically and culturally. The several hundreds of faces were such a blur from the tears that flooded his face.

Being a sensitive young man was one of his weaknesses, as the world saw it, but D.J. always counted it as strength. He enjoyed that about himself. It was one of the reasons that he would be able to put so much heart into his singing.

Every note that the band played was an imprint of a moment that had touched his soul. D.J. felt that he had to hurry to his seat before he fainted.

His only known flaw that he admitted to was not having found some meaningful relationship. He had been on a couple of one-night stands but never a love to call his own. School and his singing had been too important to him. No one else had successfully been able to get inside of his head or his heart.

The breeze that brushed the stadium was a warm welcome to D.J. It seemed to cool him off as well as dry the tears from the morning, when his parents called to say that they were going to be late. D.J. couldn't call to see where they were in the middle of the commencement, and his dad was old school and knew nothing about using text messages.

As the commencement speaker began to speak, D.J. put the thoughts out of his mind. His parents were grown, and they were probably sitting in the stands among the crowd. The speaker went on and on, and it seemed that he would never stop the sermon. He sounded more like a Baptist preacher than a motivational speaker. During the height of the speech, a chancellor and a couple of policemen seemed to be walking toward D.J. As they got closer, D.J.

knew that something was wrong. He could feel it. Why would they bring notice to themselves by walking through the ranks of graduates to find him?

"Mr. Dexton Cummings?" The chancellor said in a whisper, trying not to disrupt the ceremony.

"Yes."

"Will you please come with us?"

"What's the problem?"

"Please come with us, young man. It is imperative."

There seemed to be something in the man's voice that shot straight through D.J. He looked uneasy and slowly got up to go with the men who appeared to be a personal escort to wherever they were going to take him.

D.J. felt like he was about to be in the midst of a drug bust, although he knew he had never even remotely tried drugs.

Trip saw what was going on, immediately, he headed out of the stands to follow the men escorting his brother. Maybe D.J. was about to get arrested, and Trip was always ready for a fight or any trouble. The men led D.J. into the building into the hall; Trip was not far behind.

"Okay, Dr. Jackson, what is going on?" Trip came into the building, out of breath from running.

"Son, you are going to have to leave this building."

The policemen started to move toward Trip.

"No, he's my brother!" D.J. stated still very unnerved.

"Oh, I am so sorry." The chancellor said.

"Look, you are scaring me. What is the problem that you would take me out of my graduation?" D.J. felt a lump in his throat, and he didn't know what the problem was.

"Mr. Cummings, I am very sorry to have to tell you this, but your parents were killed in a car accident just a while ago."

"What, what are you talking about? What happened?"

I know that this is a devastating way to find out, but I didn't know what else to do.

"This is Officer Hatfield and Officer McKneely. They......"

14

Nothing else that Mr. Jackson said was penetrating D.J.'s brain. All he could hear was his brother screaming, and all he felt was his own limp body as it slid to the floor from the shock. What was he going to do? How was he going to make it? Somehow, he was able to get to his brother and comfort him.

"Come on, Trip, it is going to be alright. Everything is going to be fine. We are going to be alright." D.J. didn't know what he was saying. He didn't know what the hell he was going to do. He didn't know what the fuck was going on, but he had to be strong for his brother. "Come on, little brother, get up. Everything is going to be alright." D.J. had been crying all day, and he never thought that for the rest of his life, this day, which was supposed to bring him so much joy, would be a permanent memory of grief and despair.

"What should we do, officers?"

"We need you to come to the station with us."

"D.J., I don't want to go, man!" Trip was crying heavily. "I can't believe this. Why is this happening, D.J.? Why is this happening?"

D.J. felt the same way that his brother did. "I don't know why this is happening, but know that we are going to get through this." D.J. ambled away with the officers with his little brother holding tightly to him.

CHAPTER TWO

• • • • • • •● ●• • • • • • •

"Precious Lord, take my hand. Lead me on and let me stand. I am tired, I am weak, I am worn.........."

    This song brought back so many memories for D.J. and Trip as the choir sang softly; it was their parent's favorite. They sat on the front row in total silence and tears, spellbound at what was actually happening. The smell of the flowers made D.J. sick to his stomach. His shirt collar felt tight around his neck as he struggled to swallow as tears crowded his cheeks and left stains in his face. The church was vast and lonely even though D.J. was sitting in a crowd of people who loved his parents. D.J. had been in this church a thousand times, and it was always a welcomed treat, but today was one day that he wished that he would never have laid eyes on this place. He knew that he would never be able to view the altar the same again as he saw his parents sleeping peacefully before the congregation of loved ones, relatives, and friends. The choir in their white and blue robes seated above the bodies of his parents looked like angels that were welcoming them home to glory.

    In a strange means, it was all stunning even though he found it hard to deal with the fact that he would never be able to hear the voices of his parents again. D.J. decided to have a double funeral to get it all over with. It didn't make sense for him, allowing this thing to linger on. D.J. loved his parents too much to go through days of funerals, and this was killing him, and especially Trip. D.J. was left to make all of the arrangements as he was old enough to take charge of his parent's affairs. Some aunts and uncles wanted to come in and take control, but D.J. was strong enough to make sure that the arrangements went the way that he thought that his parents would have wanted them to be.

D.J. wished that he could turn back the hands of time. He thought that everything was going to be remarkable in his life. D.J. flashed back to the day he went to the mailbox, and there he found an envelope that held the degree he had worked so hard for. Inside was his degree, and to his surprise, there was a personal letter from the president of the university. D.J. read the letter in complete awe and appreciation that he would even be thought of.

"It is with the deepest regret but a joyful heart that I send this to you. I know that the last couple of days have been hard, but we, as a school family, would like to extend our deepest condolences to you and your family. I hope this degree is not a reminder of sorrow, but confirmation of hope for brighter days. If there is anything that I can do for you, please feel free to personally contact me.

Humbly,
Zachariah Toldson, President"

D.J. had just received his degree that was supposed to promise nothing but happiness, but here he was at one of the lowest moments he had ever experienced. Things couldn't be any worse than they were at that moment. He sat on the curb teary-eyed, wondering if he would be able to breathe another minute.

D.J. immediately snapped back into reality and remembered where he was. He wanted to run out the back of the church and never turn around, but he knew it was not the thing to do.

D.J. walked up the podium to speak about his amazing parents. As he scanned over the crowd, he could only focus on the deep green eyes of his baby brother, who seemed to be the only one he could connect too. The black suit he was dressed in made him look like a younger version of his father.

As he began to speak, he felt a strength that comes from somewhere that seemed to hold him up. He spoke as best he could of the two individuals who had given his life purpose. Shortly afterward, he opened his mouth to sing, *"When I get to heaven."* As the tears fell into the lapel of his suit, he sang in the hopes that his parents would hear him as they walked into the pearly gates.

After everyone left the gravesite, D.J. was still there staring at the uneven ground of which held the bodies of the two people who he loved more than anything in life itself. There were flowers everywhere. The gravesite seemed like a garden that offered the most beautiful flowers of every type. As the wind blew lightly, D.J. knew that he would never forget the smell of those flowers. Trip went home with Aunt Kandiest, where they would be staying a couple of days. D.J. was not ready to go at the time, and his relatives understood. He had a lot of things to think through, and he could not focus on the people around him. As the gentle breeze cooled the warm tears that fell from his face, he heard comforting voices in the background.

"D.J., how are you doing, man?" Ped' east said.

"Hello, my brother," Kendall spoke softly after Ped' east.

D.J. turned and saw his brothers. They always put a smile on his face, even though his world was torn in two. As the fellas walked closer, D.J. began to wipe his eyes as not to show the pain that was continually ripping at his very being.

"What's up, fellas?" D.J. tried to produce a slight smile, but it seemed like one of the hardest things that he could do at that moment.

"Hey man, you don't have to be strong for us. We came here to be with you in your time of sorrow." Kendall said. The three men embraced each other. Even though Kendall and Ped' east had not gone to the same school as D.J., they never ceased from being the best of friends and staying in contact with each other. "I don't know what I am going to do, fellas. I feel like my world is coming to an end. What am I going to do?" D.J. started to cry, and his brothers instantly hugged him.

"Look, you don't have to walk this thing by yourself. You know that you have both of us. We are your family and don't you forget that." D.J. looked up to see Kendall crying. Ped' east was caught in the moment, but no tears had fallen from his eyes.

"I tell you what you need to do," Kendall said to D.J. "You need to come with me and Ped' east to New York just like we planned. I know you don't want to think about this now, but your parents would love for you to continue with your life."

"Man, are you crazy? I can't go to New York. What do you think that I am going to be able to do with my little brother?" D.J. said, a little upset.

"I know that you have relatives who can take care of him until you can get yourself and your career together." Ped' east said a little upset.

"Look, maybe I did not make myself clear in my last statement, but I am not going to New York. I am the only one who is left to take care of my brother, and I will not leave him here after having lost both of our parents."

"Hey, calm down, man. We don't mean to upset you. You know that we would give our right arms for you." Kendall said, smiling at D.J., hoping that he would smile back. D.J. paused for a moment. He knew that his boys would never say or do anything to hurt him. Hell, they had been best friends for years. He knew they only wanted what was best for him, and that was something that he could bank on.

"Okay, dudes, I ain't trippin'. Today has just been a terrible day for me."

"We know man, but every day is going to be easier, and you are going to be fine." Kendall said. Ped' east was nodding his head in agreement. Ped' east held up his scarred finger. "One for all!" D.J. and Kendall placed their thumbs to meet with Ped' east. "And all for one." D.J. and Kendall said in unison. The brothers led D.J. away from the gravesite, knowing that although today was rough for D.J., he would eventually come around.

Several weeks passed, and D.J. and Trip were sitting in D.J.'s bedroom, talking. "D.J., look. I know that you don't think that I can take care of myself, but I can. I only have one year of high school left, and you know that Aunt Kandiest won't let me do anything that I am not supposed to do. You know just as well as I do that I am in good hands."

"I know, but I would worry about you too much."

"You are so fucking stupid! I think that you should take your ass to New York. You know the moment that I graduate, I am on my way there anyway. It's only one year. We both have the destiny to fulfill, and it will be time to get my hands on some new punanay." Trip said with a smile.

"See, that is what I am talking about. Who is going to be here to keep your little hormones in check?"

"Look, I promise to repent, every time I get up out of the booty!" Trip was starting to act stupid now. He got down on his knees and put his hands in prayer position. D.J. knew that it was a losing battle. "I know that you think that I am stupid, but I really want you to understand that I can take care of myself. You taught me that. Even though mom and dad meant the world to me, it was you who taught me everything that I know. Now, if I fail, it is because you didn't teach me right." Trip knew that would bring a smile to D.J.'s face.

"You are a stupid little person, but you have a good head on your shoulders."

"Hey baby, I learned from the best."

D.J. got up and gave his little brother a big hug. Hugging his brother at that point comforted Trip, even though he always said that he didn't like it. He loved his big brother, and he needed that hug. They enjoyed the relationship they had, even though Trip had the filthiest mouth in creation. That was something that D.J. was still working on with him and probably would never win the battle.

D.J. sat on the front step of his apartment building. He had been in New York for some time now, but he was still grieved with being lonely. He did find some comfort with sitting out on the step, breathing in the new atmosphere around him. It was so different from Baton Rouge or Atlanta. It was funny to see kids really playing in the water of the fire hydrant that was opened by a badass little boy who was pushed up by the other kids to do it.

It was hot, but the heat was dry, and it didn't make you sweat like the humid climate of Louisiana. There were parents shouting out of the window.

Words like, "Jonathan bring yo black ass in here and clean up this damn room!" This whole place was so different, but D.J. was excited about being there, and at the same time, he was lonely as hell.

He was on an emotional roller coaster. He knew that it was time to get his career started, but he also missed his brother desperately. Although they talked every day, he still felt as though he had abandoned him after only a few weeks after they had buried both of their parents. He knew that life was different. He just had no idea if it would turn out good or bad. Some days he felt like he was having a nervous breakdown. For the first time in his life, he could neither hear the music in his head nor could he feel it pulsating through his veins. He wondered if it was only for a short time, or would he never know the pleasure of music that was the true beat of his heart. Hell, maybe it was time to really be a man and find a job. Perhaps it was just time to grow up. D.J.'s mind was so clouded with grief and guilt of his brother he didn't know if he would ever smile again.

Part Two:

The Reunion

CHAPTER THREE

Trip, looking at the scar on his index finger, reminiscing over the backyard sleepover. It seemed like only yesterday he and his blood brothers made the decision to pursue their dreams of stardom. Trip lay back in his thoughts as he listened to the sounds of Mint Condition from his headset. The clouds from the airplane window seemed to form magical pictures of animated characters as the plane whizzed through them. Trip was the last of the pack to take the voyage to New York City. Even though he was younger than the rest of the guys and not a college graduate, he knew that he would be welcomed by the fellas who he had followed all of his life.

December 31, 1998, marked the day that officially the group would be complete once again. A year and three months prior, both parents of Trip and D.J. were killed in a car accident. D.J. wanted Trip to come to N.Y. right afterward, but there were some things Trip had to take care of. He needed some time to put closure on his life in Baton Rouge. Trip realized although the occasion was sad, this would be the best moment for him to finally join the rest of the pack. Big brother would give him a place to stay as long as he needed. He figured he could get his life started in dancing. Trip had taken every kind of class and style of dance there was to name. He knew the more versatile he was, the better he would be able to market himself one day. Modern, Tap, Ballet, Jazz, and his favorite Hip-hop were his past times.

Even though the fellas used to call him a sissy, he knew what he wanted for his life, and he cared what no one thought when it came to his craft. Trip knew he had the moves. He was teaching a hip-hop class at the Y and, over the years, gathered a nice crowd of people who took his class. He even taught a hip-hop aerobics class, and the older women seemed to love that.

Most of the time, Trip just believed that the ladies liked his piercing green eyes. Trip had very exotic features that were passed on to him from his great-grandfather. The almond skin, the high cheekbones, and the cat green eyes gave him advantages to things, especially the ladies, that others could not even imagine possible. The combination of his striking great looks, his lean, toned body, and his extraordinary dance moves, Trip was ready to give New York City everything he had to offer. He had done a few things in Louisiana, and now it was time for him to move it to a new level, the league of the "big boys," and it was either swim or sink.

The stewardess handed Trip a glass of apple juice and some mixed nuts as he gazed out of the window, thinking about the pack's lives and how he was going to fit in with them. Trip had a tremendous high school life, not so much academically, but he was a social superstar: he had many friends, the ladies loved him, the jokester, and the teachers' pet. Life had been actually satisfying to him, although he was a screw-up. People always thought that they would be able to talk with him and get him on the right track. Trip would always say that he was going to do the right thing. He would flash that perfect smile, cured by five thousand dollars' worth of braces, at them and wink with those "drop dead" eyes, and everyone would believe that he was all right.

There were times when he was unsure of himself and his place in the world. Even though Trip had many friends, it was the pack that was his strong shoulders that helped him through some of the toughest times of his life. The day D.J. left, Trip sat in the window for three solid hours, hoping he was coming back around the corner back into his life.

Kendall and Ped' east had gone to Grambling on scholarships—Kendall on a football scholarship and Ped' east for the band. Kendall was a natural athlete, but in his sophomore year in college, he tore his ACL (anterior cruciate ligament), and his football days were over. Though distraught, after finally getting the playing time he deserved, he had the perfect opportunity to change his major from physical therapy to his first love, theater. Of course, Kendall was great at acting. He went on to perform great dramas for the university, and his range of acting grew tremendously. He continued to work out and even took a job as a bouncer on weekends to stay in shape. Kendall knew his life was destined to be a successful actor, but his father didn't see the excitement in a 185-pound power machine as an actor. Kendall's father was from a different mindset, and he thought the acting and those kinds of things were for "sissies." He saw the potential Kendall had, early in his little league life as an athlete, and guided his youngest son toward a career in sports. His father proudly carried several of his newspaper clippings in his wallet and would pull them out and show them to everyone that would stand still long enough for him to show them off. After the injury and the two major surgeries, Ken's father, realizing that his career was practically over, started to call less and took no part in his new life as an actor. In one major argument about his needing money to pay his college fees, all Kendall remembered was leaving the house and his father shouting at him,

"You always did have a hard-ass head boy, but if you make your bed hard, then you damn sure gon' have to lie in it."

"Whateva Pop! I am so tired of having to live my life supporting your dream of being an "NFL" father. I am doing what I do for me."

"Go ahead, then, take yo ass on out there and do something with cha self, but I ain't giving you a rusty ass penny! You hear me, not a penny!
Kendall walked away in tears mumbling under his breath, *"You never did, Pops, anyway, you never did!"*

Kendall was out to prove his father wrong. He didn't know how he was going to do it, but if it took the rest of his life, he was going to do it. But he had to start by taking out a loan to finish school.

Ped' east went to Grambling on a band scholarship but spent most of his time securing and developing a spot as a campus radio personality. After realizing an apparent conflict with the band and his ambitions, he found his career in radio broadcasting and producing was much more critical; so he gave up the band. He later became a campus favorite and was asked to emcee several campus functions. His hour of power was a welcomed treat during the "seven to eleven" hour. Affectionately known as the "trouble maker." He got his name from the mellow R&B he played on his show seemed to send young couples into sexual overdrive. It was rumored his show had become "the lovemaking hours!" Ped' east became a campus celebrity, and his ego had somewhat started to make him think he was actually a star.

Both finished Grambling the spring of the same year—Kendall in Liberal Arts/Theatrics and Ped' east in Mass Communications/ Radio Broadcasting.

Trip lay with his head back on his seat and noticed that the flight attendant was staring at him. I guess she could not believe that with his skin color, he could have eyes as deep green as they were.

"Yes, they are real." Trip said, noticing that she had never taken her eyes off him. She approached him biting on his bottom lip.

"Please excuse me for staring, but you are so damn handsome."

"Thank you. I'm Trip."

"Well, hello Trip, I'm Katrina."

"Nice to meet you, Katrina."

Trip really was not used to this small talk, but he figured he should start as he was on his way to a new place, and if this is how they did it, well, he may as well learn the ropes.

"Please forgive me for being forward, but you are probably the finest thang I have ever seen on this airline."

"Are you flirting with me, Katrina?"

"Is it working?"

"Yes, it is!" Trip was not used to ladies being so forward with him. He was used to those knuckle-headed tricks that frequented his high school and in the surrounding neighborhood so "hitting that ass and moving on" was something he did well. But this was different.

"You are strikingly beautiful yourself. What are you doing after this plane lands?

"I'm on a return flight, but we can talk more in the back if you like."

"Trip noticed that she never took her eyes off him. It was like she was memorized or something. It should have been a little awkward, but it wasn't. I guess Trip was a little freakier than he thought.

"I bet you talk sweet like this to all the guys you meet on these planes." Trip said with a slight smile.

"Nah, usually I am so much more reserved, but you are beautiful. If you can say that a man is beautiful."

Trip laughed "It's all good. I'll take that compliment. You are even more beautiful. I bet we could make some cute babies."

Katrina started smiling. "Humph, cute, sexy, and knows how to flatter a woman," she said.

"More than you know. I got a little foolishness in me too."

"Really now?" "How old are you, Trip?"

"Old enough to be legal everywhere, even at thirty-six thousand feet." Trip said in his deep southern vernacular.

She started to the back of the plane with inviting eyes, and after a couple of seconds, Trip got up and followed the provocative woman. Does shit like this really happen? Am I about to be a member of the mile-high club? Trip really wasn't that sure of what it was, but he heard about it from older people as he was ear hustling on their conversations. Trip smiled to himself. This is one grand graduation gift. He grinned from ear to ear. Trip slipped in the back restroom of the plane. Katrina was already in there. The space was small, but there was more than enough room for Trip to "tap that ass" quickly before anyone knew what was happening. Katrina already had her skirt up and her red lace thong was showing. As Trip was unbuckling his pants, she dropped to her knees to take him fully into her mouth. Trip's long arms gripped each side of the walls to steady himself from the plane's slight turbulence. Katrina's slurping sounds was music to his ears as he pushed forward forcefully to deliver every bit of him into her warm throat. After a few moments, she stood up, lifted one leg, pulled her thong to the side, slipped a condom on him and mounted Trip. He was trying not to moan, but the surprise of it all, the fear of getting caught, and the moist feeling he felt from inside her, made him love it even more. She placed her hand over his mouth, and it made Trip more excited and he side-rolled his hips to fit every bit of him into her while releasing a quiet moan. Katrina never took her eyes off those deep emeralds. Trip didn't know what hit him. Was this flight attendant really that freaky? She had to have done this before. No woman could be this good in this small space without having some knowledge of the dimensions of this tight room to maximize full pleasure and had not done this before. Nevertheless, Trip held one of her breasts in one hand (as she held the other) and the other around her waist in order to hold her up and dig deeper into her "punanay" as he called it. A few more pumps and grunts and he exploded. She tightened to let Trip know that she was cummin' as well. After the quickie was over, they both cleaned up and each went back to what they were previously doing; Trip watching the clouds and Katrina's faint voice a few feet back saying "peanuts, water, coffee, sir?" "Damn!" Trip thought. "That was fire. The boys are never gonna believe this shit?" Once again he lay his head back and drifted away into the clouds with visions of Katrina and the new experience on his mind.

As the plane was taxiing into the runway, Trip's heart started to pace faster. In his mind, he had played this scene a thousand times. He knew his brothers would accept him, but that still did not stop his feelings of nervousness. Trip brushed his hands across the top of his hair, took a deep breath, and joined the line of people exiting the plane. One last glimpse of Katrina with a slight grin, a returned wink from her, and Trip exited the plane. Damn, he forgot to even get a number or something so that he could see to talk to her again. Oh well, maybe it was not meant to be. Sometimes the moment is just that…just a moment.

LaGuardia's airport was huge. It was nothing like the airport that he knew. There were so many terminals that he didn't know if he would be able to find his way to the outside. Would this entire city overwhelm him just like this airport? Trip turned around to the best site he had seen in years. Grinning from ear to ear, the sight of the brothers he had not seen in years almost brought tears to his eyes. He didn't realize how much he had missed the big brothers of his life.

"Stupid, what's up" Ped' east joked as usual. Ped' east had not changed a bit, and Trip was glad.

"Hey, fellas, what's up?" Trip said.

"Nothing, little man, how's it hanging?" Kendall said. "I got your hangin', and it's hangin' to the left!" Trip laughingly said to Kendall.

"Still got that filthy mouth, huh, boy?" Ped' east said.

"Sure as hell do, and as long as I can breathe, I will always have it!" Trip knew this was not Baton Rouge, but he would do his best to make this place home. He knew the pack would help him to make the transition. The four guys headed toward the baggage claim and then out of the airport into the New York air. They were on their way to the "Purple Tiger," a favorite spot of the guys when they decided to get together. The ride over was grand. They chatted about things of the past, the present things they had done, and they talked about the future.

"Man, Ped' east, I see you're still holding on to your mama's nipple. It must have some damn good milk in it. I know that she bought you this Navigator." Trip said to Ped' east with a smirk.

"Now, come on, fool, don't play with me, and don't play yourself!" Ped' east was doing well for himself without his parent's help. He had landed himself a job in production for WRIA. He had worked his way up to a substitute radio host when the regulars could not make it into work. A big producer of the company happened to be listening in on one of the shows he hosted, liked his style, and the rest is history. Although he was not making the big bucks, he was doing well for himself. As a second job, he was an amateur producer, but he did have two strong talents under his small company.

They pulled up to the restaurant, and the valet took the keys. Trip was amazed at the clout that Ped' east had. He had really come up. At the table, the fellows went on to talk about the things they encountered during their stay in New York.

"A toast to the pack's reunion!" D.J. said. Taking their glasses in one hand, they suddenly remembered the way they ended all gatherings together by placing their sacred index fingers in the air and letting them meet high in the center.

"So, are we really planning on getting the group back together?" Trip said naively. The other guys chuckled to themselves. They had come to the reality that even though they had fulfilled their dreams of making it to New York, maturity and life lead them down totally different career paths.

"Sorry, little brother, I am the only one of us is trying to hold a flame in the singing arena," D.J. said. Ped' east was pursuing his dreams of radio and producing artists, and Kendall was struggling, but a devoted actor. Although Kendall had experienced several downfalls amid his career, he had landed several commercials that kept him paying his bills. He also held a mini-role on a popular daytime soap opera.

The fellas continued their evening in bliss. They were happy Trip had joined them. It was just like old times. The characteristics of each of them, although they were older and wiser, was still the same. The pack was still the pack.

CHAPTER FOUR

· · · · · · ● ● ● ● ● ● ● ● · · · · ·

Trip woke up in the soft comfort of his brother's guest room. Trip felt his head beaming as he pulled himself from the bed and into the hallway. As he walked down the hallway, he faintly enjoyed the black art that covered his brother's wall. It seemed to Trip that the brothers were doing their thang in this city. He could smell the breakfast, just like in the old times, and he knew that big brother was near.

"Good morning, little brother."

"Not so loud, man, good morning."

"It is almost twelve o'clock. I thought that you were not going to ever wake up."

"Well, you should not have kept me out so late."

"Well, I thought that you could hang," D.J. said with a smirk.

"Come on, man, you are still talking too loud."

"Hey, little brother, I have to go out for a while, but I should be back in a couple of hours."

"Okay, I guess that I will just eat, and go back to bed, hopefully, I will be up when you get back."

As D.J. headed out of the door, Trip turned on the T.V. and flopped back into the comfort of the old leather couch with the homemade booty prints his brother had made and finished off his breakfast. Before he knew it, he was again deep into a peaceful trance.

Kendall lay in his bed, weary from the night before. He always had a great time with his old friends. Being with the fellows made him forget about all of his problems. Problems so hard for him that he could not even share with the pack. Although Kendall had done some great things since he had been in New York, the gigs were so far an in-between that the bills were coming around faster than the money was coming in. In purchasing his condominium and his car, he had not considered that his acting career was not as steady as he wanted it to be, so the bills were starting to pile up. This was why he took a job at the "Solar Fitness" gym. Being a past athlete and his beautiful physique landed him the job. The boss could not resist when she saw his resume, but better yet, the shirt that outlined his every hard muscle. Although Kendall wanted more acting jobs, he found that he could keep in shape and continue to pay the bills working at the gym. It also helped him to ease the stress and anxiety of life that always seemed to interrupt his day.

Kendall got up to check his answering machine as he turned on the shower to get ready to go to the gym for the morning.

"Hey, Ken, this is Keisha, I missed you last night, give me a call when you get a chance."

Beep

"Yo, K, man, we need you at the gym earlier if you can get here. Hit me back at the office."

Beep

"Kendall, this is D.J., I hope that you are alright. I know that you were wasted last night, and I was just checking on you. Give me a call when you get a chance."

Kendall walked to the fridge, grabbed a swig of tomato juice, and headed off toward the shower. Today was going to be a long and exhausting day.

By the time that Kendall reached the gym, it was loaded with people. It was indeed a place that people could enjoy. There was light music playing in the background, and there were large-screen televisions in every room.

"What is up, Kendall? Jason said. Jason was one of the other physical trainers at the gym.

Jason was also one who was stacked with muscles. Kim, the manager, planned it that way. She wanted the ladies satisfied with the eye candy and the gentlemen wanting their bodies, so this way, everyone would keep coming back. Jason was very in tune with his body and what it took to keep it in shape. He had even been in some amateur bodybuilding competitions. The women who frequented there loved the view of the sexy men who were at their beck and call.

"Nothing is going on, man, I don't have any that I can complain about." The fellas high-fived each other as they went about their day's activities.

The atmosphere of the gym was one that those that could afford it could really enjoy it. Beautiful women of all races seemed to smile at Kendall as he passed by them.

"Hey, Ken," said one of the young ladies.

"Hey ladies, y'all looking good!" Ken smiled back.

Ken made his way over to the women who he would be training. Ken loved his job as a personal trainer. It was a great way to meet women.

"Hey Kendall, I didn't think that you would be in this early."

"Of course, I would be here, you know that I would not miss a moment to watch you in action."

"Come on now, don't tease me, you know that I might just have to take you home." Kendall knew how to flatter the women no matter what size they were.

"And I would let you too, as long as you will be gentle with me," Kendall said as he winked at the young lady.

"I see that you have been doing a little bit of working before I got here," Ken said as he checked the lady's chart.

"Yeah, I feel a little bit more energy today than usual. At that moment, one of Kendall's commercials came across the television.

"You look good, is this a new commercial?"

"No, I did this one a couple of months ago. Thanks for the compliment."

Hours passed, and the gym was starting to wind down.

Kendall was taking a break when he heard a voice coming up behind him.

"Ken, my man, how are you doing?" Ken turned around to a slick, well-dressed man that everyone called "Deacon."

"Hey, what's up, man? I see that you have been here trying to get your swole on."

"Yeah, I tried to do a little something, something." Deacon said with a sly grin. "Hey, my man, I want to talk with you about a little something? If you have a minute."

"Go ahead, Deac, I'm listening."

"I heard that you were having a little money drought, and I know that you are a great actor, so I thought I would bring a little business your way."

"Who told you that?" Kendall said with a sharp eye.

"Hey, does all that really matter? I'm here to help you to throw a little business your way."

"What kind of business are you talking about"?

"Well, I own a little acting company, and I thought you would be interested in working for me."

"What kind of company is it?"

"Well, I won't lie to you; it is in the adult film industry and with your body…" Kendall never let him finish a sentence.

"Man, have you lost your fucking mind? Do I look like some sort of freak to you."?

"Look, I didn't mean to offend you, but maybe you can…"

"Case closed, it is time for you to go." Kendall seemed to get angrier at every word. "I don't get down like that, and I don't show my shit to the world."

"Well, brother, if you change your mind, here is my card."

"You are really trying to piss me off! Look! The gym is closing, and I suggest that you leave." Deacon gave in to Kendall's commands and left quietly without saying another word.

Kendall yawned as he looks up at the clock and finds that it is now 1:30 a.m. He has finished straightening up his area and is the last one left to lock up the gym. He replayed his conversation with Deacon a thousand times. Ken decided that he would relax in the sauna before going home. He went to the locker to undress. As the locker door opened it, one of Deacon's cards fell out of it.

"That slick bastard, he never gives up," Kendall thought to himself as he picked up the card and threw it into his locker. He quickly undressed, wrapped himself in a towel, and grabbed his baby oil before heading to the sauna. The coolness of the floor tingled his manly pedicured feet. As he stepped into the quiet wetness of the sauna room, the steamy warmness was a calming relaxation from the tiring day's events.

Kendall released the towel from his sculpted body and placed it across the wooden seat to lay in full freedom. The haze of the damp fog gave him a mist of seclusion, which furthered his feeling of openness. Ken began to massage the baby oil into his skin. The combination of oil and steam delicately trickled from his slightly hairy chest and warmly fell into his pubic area. His sex seemed to arouse as he thought about the escapades he encountered in his life. Maybe he could be a porn star? Naw, he knew that his mother wouldn't allow it, and his grandmother would turn over in her grave if she even thought that he would do such a thing. Oddly enough, he was flattered by Deac's proposition and the possibility of enjoying beautiful women as they probed and caressed his body. Kendall began to slowly and smoothly caress the baby oil onto his uncircumcised penis, feeling it harden with each silky, wet touch. Before he knew it, he was caught up in his stroke and the sensation of unsheltered lust. With his free hand, Kendall ran his fingers across the baby smooth hair that lay across his chest, creating a feeling that only he could bring to himself. Vivid pictures of voluptuous women flashed before him as he began to pick up the stroke of his manhood. Kendall poured more baby oil into his lower region to magnify the feeling of warm simulated femininity. He felt a volcano in him begging to overflow, and with an uninhibited grunt, he erupted.

In an instant, Kendall's chest was covered with milky white satisfaction. Embarrassed, yet overwhelmed with lust and a slight smile, he decided to take a shower, go home, and give Cheryl a call. She was always a booty call in waiting.

Part Three:

Six Months Later

CHAPTER FIVE

· · · · · · ●●● ● ●●● · · · · · ·

Trip sat in the smoke-filled club in full amazement. He had now been in New York City for six months but had not been to see what his brother did best. There seemed to be some notable people at this establishment. It appeared to Trip that D.J. already hit the big time.

"Hey, little brother, you made it."

"Yeah, man, I told you I was coming."

"Good, let me get you something to drink, my treat."

"Alright then, I have a whiskey sour."

"What, I was thinking more like a cranberry twist!"

"Do I look like a punk to you, come on man, I'm nineteen and will be twenty in a couple of months."

"Okay, cool, I'll get it for you, but don't think that this is about to become a habit!"

"Yes, father, I have sinned, please forgive me?" Trip said sarcastically.

"I know you are a man, but I still worry about your Lil' scrawny ass."

"Scrawny? Please, women, love these muscles, and I like to let them touch 'em." Trip started flexing his muscles.

D.J. was about to go into his fatherly mode when he heard the band start, and he knew this was his cue.

"Be back in a sec, cat eyes, enjoy the show." D.J. ran up on stage.

The slow groove of the band seemed to set the atmosphere. People, who were having quiet conversations, suddenly seemed to cease as D.J. let the audience have it with an original piece that he wrote.

"People are always chasing rainbows...looking for pie in the sky. But my guide to the treasure is you girl, yes you girl!" D.J.'s voice ran across the smoky fog of the bar room. The ladies seemed to be at awe of how the background music was a perfect accent to his silky, smooth voice. Even the fellows knew that the more D.J. sang, the better their chances would be of "getting a little somethin', somethin'!" or least later on that night. Trip loved to hear his brother sing. He sat back in his seat with his head up, and his chest poked out like anyone would know he was even kin to the brother on stage.

Trip sat through the entire show of his brother without even blinking. It had been such a long time since he had last listened to his brother.

After the set, D.J. came back to the table. Trip had a huge grin on his face.

"What are you so happy about?" D.J. said.

"Nothing, man! I just haven't heard you sing in a long time." Trip said, "I see you still got it."

"I do my best!" D.J. said, slightly bragging.

In an instant, a beautiful woman walked into the club, and Trip almost choked on his drink.

"Who is that?" Trip said.

"Hey, you want me to introduce you? Her name is Shanique, she works the late shift."

"I sure would like to work her late shift!" Trip said seductively.

"Stop trippin', she is a good woman, but she has three kids and is divorced."

"Man down, turn off," Trip grunted.

"Stop it, she's sweet, and besides, she didn't ask to be your friend."

By this time, the disc jockey had belted out one of Trip's favorite songs. Before D.J. could finish his sentence, Trip got up and made his way to the floor. D.J. had the voice, but Trip had the moves. By his first thirty seconds on the dance floor, Trip was already dancing with two women. His rhythm and personality set the dance floor on fire. Trip was the type of dancer that really didn't need a partner. He could have a great time by himself. Each song after that found Trip in a frenzy of excitement. New York was finally starting to feel like home.

"Happy New Year, fellas," D.J. said. It had just struck twelve, and he was just a little bit tipsy.

"You always got to say some corny shit, don't you? Can't we just sit out here and drink like real men? Please don't start acting like white people!"

"And you always got something stupid to say, and it is always followed by some cuss words," Kendall said to Trip.

"You damn skippy!" Trip said.

"Y'all know that nigga ain't gon' change," Ped' east said.

All of the men started to laugh. It seemed like nothing had changed within the circle of friends. Even though the place and the scene changed, the fellas were still the same. Their physical features were much different, but their ideas of brotherhood were the same. They still enjoyed each other's company. The men sat around for hours talking doing nothing special but enjoying the brotha's night out, bringing in and celebrating the New Year.

"Hey fellas, are we gon' sit around here all night, or are there any freaks out there waiting on us" Trip said.

"Why don't you just shut up, boy?" D.J. said.

"Naw D.J., I agree with Lil' stupid this time. I love hanging with the boys, but I think it is time to say goodnight and bring the morning in with a little New Year's booty! Ped' east said while rubbing his hands together.

"See, big brother, I told you that I wasn't the only freak!" Trip laughed.

"Whateva dudes, y'all niggas get out and go handle your business, but I am going to get some bed action too, but trust me. It will be nothing but sleeping in for the rest of the New Year." D.J. started to yawn.

"A'ight, let's holla a little later," Kendall said, getting up and walking toward the door. As the fellas left, D.J. looked around his crib at the mess the pack had left behind. He grabbed the last beer off the table and went out onto the balcony.

The city lights from across the way was a beautiful sight for him. New York was a special place to be, and D.J. knew it. He finally got his mojo back. New York was beginning to feel like home.

Trip woke up the next morning to the sound of the telephone ring. He called for D.J. to answer it, but he didn't seem to hear him fumbling around. As the phone rang again, Trip fell out of bed, trying to answer the phone.

"Hello, who the hell is this calling this time of the morning?" Trip yawned into the phone.

"What's up, you little shit! This is Ped' east. Hey, I got a hook up for you."

"Yeah, yeah, what is it!" Trip said, yawning on the phone.

"I'm serious man, I have a hook up you don't want to miss."

"Okay, man, spit it out! You're too old for this shit!" Trip seemed to be getting agitated.

"Okay, I'll tell you. I got you an audition in a new video with Joya Reynolds. Your audition is today at 3:30 p.m. It's at the Clark building on Ontario and Dubois, so get your ass up and shower." Ped' east knew he had excited Trip, and that was his business, making clients into stars. Although Trip was not one of his clients, he was still one of the pack, and it was their code to help each other in need.

"Cool man, I am all over it. I'll talk with you later." Trip said

"Alright man, peace."

"Hey, Ped' east."

"Yeah."

"Thanks, man!"

"Hey, I would do anything for those pretty green eyes."

"Fuck you, dude, talk to you tonight."

Trip jumped out of bed with what seemed a new burst of energy. He sang his way to the shower and turned the water on. As he undressed in front of the mirror, he began to flex. He knew that he had "the look." He was not afraid to tell himself that. His lean frame full of muscles and his broad smile with two hard dimples and, of course, deep green eyes made even the coldest women melt. Trip had the swag, and he knew it.

Trip made it to the audition an hour before it started. There was a line of people he saw curved around the corner. He didn't mind standing in the line because he knew his talent and also had a hookup, so it was just a matter of time before the inevitable happened. Trip found comfort in a girl who was in front of him. She heard about the audition and traveled all the way from Toronto. Trip smiled to himself as he thought about all of the people, like himself, who had a dream they intended to pursue, no matter the distance or the cost. It took little under an hour for Trip to make it to the front of the line. The wait calmed him down, even though it should have made him more nervous. The friendly conversation from the interesting young lady made the time pass faster. Trip entered the cold front office room. "Man! He thought to himself, so this is what is it like on the inside of an audition place." He informed the lady at the front desk of his name, she checked his name on her list, and then she immediately guided him down a narrow hall to the studio. Trip could hear the sounds of hip-hop music coming from the inside of the room he was approaching, and he was dying to get in there. As he entered the room, a thin, but muscular man glistening in sweat greeted him. The man wiped his sweat with his towel. Trip introduced himself to the man.

"So you are Trip?" The man said, "I heard a lot about you! I heard that you were the bomb. My friend Ped' east says you are really on your shit," the man said.

"I do a'ight," Trip said with a sly grin.

"Okay, then Mr. Modest, show me what you got," the man said.

Trip wasn't sure if the guy was being sarcastic or not, but he knew what he could do, and he was sure of that. There were about fifteen people in the room, mostly dancers and maybe a few bigwigs in suits, but they didn't bother Trip. This was the moment that he had been waiting for. He put his bag on the floor, nearest the door, and walked toward the center of the glass-encircled room. Trip gave the guy his music. The music started, and Trip started doing his thing. This city was used to hearing reggae, but Trip was about to bring them some "dirty, down south" love. A mixture of hip-hop, funk, and original modern choreography was what he threw at them. As usual, the combination of his smooth moves, and that face of his, captivated those watching. After two minutes of dancing, Trip knew that he had him in his palm.

When the music stopped, the people in the room started to clap. He saw the young lady who he talked to in the line outside. She gave him a quick "thumbs up," He blew a small innocent kiss at her. Out of breath, but totally excited, Trip walked over to the man.

"What do you think?" Trip said, knowing he had impressed the guy.

"Not bad, not bad," The man said, rubbing his chin. "But, let's see how you do with some choreography that isn't yours."

The choreographer signaled for everyone standing along the wall to come and be a part of the routine he had been teaching them before Trip came in. "Five, six, seven, eight!" The man started three eight counts of some fast-paced moves, and Trip paid careful attention to what they were doing. He knew that he had to be on top of his game to hang with the "big dawgs." When the count started again, Trip jumped in with passion. He made every move precisely as he had been shown. The choreographer added in six more eight counts, and the class was back up to full speed. They were in the middle of the dance, and Trip was "tearing it down." At that moment, Joya Reynolds walked in. Heads began to turn, but he was in a zone, and he kept his mind on his dance. Trip didn't notice she had walked in. When the music stopped, Trip was dog tired, yet he felt exhilarated. He walked toward the door to retrieve the bottle of water from his bag. It was then that he caught eyes with Joya Reynolds.

"You got some good moves, boy," Joya said.

"Thanks, ma'am" Trip smiled back at her.

"Ma'am, I know that you did not just call me ma'am? Do I look like someone's grandmother," Joya said jokingly.

"I'm sorry, I'm tripping. Thank you for the compliment."

"So, what is your name?" she said.

"Trip is my name." He giggled.

"Are you trying to be funny?"

"Nope, that's my name, why don't you like it?" Trip said, starting to get his confidence back.

"Yeah, I like it, as well as those beautiful green eyes of yours."

"Well, if you like the eyes, you're gonna love the dimples," Trip said, tilting his head slightly.

"Oh, you got jokes? I guess you think you are all of that?"

"No, not all that, but most of it!"

They both smiled at the same time.

Trip could not believe he was having a casual conversation with Joya Reynolds. By this time, several bigwigs came to talk with her about one thing or another. The choreographer told Trip he would hear from them in a couple of days. Trip grabbed his things and walked out. His day could not have gone better if he had prayed about it. This was definitely a lookup.

CHAPTER SIX

· · · · · · · ●● ● ●● · · · · · · ·

Ped' east slid the strawberry across the back of her neck. Monet' moaned in pleasure. Monet' was one of the production assistants at the radio station. She had been showing signs for months; she was interested in him.. Finally, the time had come that Ped' east would give her what she had been asking for, and more. Monet' laid on her back, and Ped' east already had her out of her shirt and bra. The soft down comforter felt like they were riding a cloud. Ped' east put her in the mood while sending her body into a frenzy. He reached around and placed the strawberry around her lips and into her mouth. He took hold of her pants from behind and pulled them gently down her leg and around her ankles. Next, he slid off her black lace panties just as passionately; he gently spread her legs, crawled up behind her, and laid his warm body on top of hers. He started breathing warmly on the neck right before beginning to nibble on her ear and then her neck. She was ready for entry. He flipped her over hard yet gentle.

Women want the man to be in control while being gentle and sensitive to their sexual needs and fantasies. Ped' east was taught this in high school by an older woman in his neighborhood whose husband was cheating on her, and she knew it. She wanted revenge but settled for a young buck she could teach the ropes and who enjoyed the training and the bragging rights. That first time was a seduction, but every time after that was a lesson in session. He was well seasoned by this time.

Ped' east grabbed another strawberry from the bowl and placed it into her mouth. He kissed her gently down her left side and then her right alternating slowly and meticulously. Her body tightened at each deliberate kiss. Before she knew it, he tasted her warm sweet juice, and fireworks went off in her head. For several minutes, he pleasured her with his long, thick tongue. Her body began to spasm; she could hold her screams no longer. Grabbing the back of Ped' east head, she plunged him deeper into her vagina. Finally, after completing his task of a well-planned foreplay, he found his way back up to her sensitive breast. He licked circles around her nipples as he raised her legs onto his shoulders. He nuzzled a little harder into her nipples to offset the surprise of his stiffness sliding into her slick yoni.

Monet' didn't know what hit her. She grabbed his ass to let him know that she was ultimately into him, diving deeper into her moist lips. Her groans of pleasure let him know he hit the spot. The right one at that! The rotation of his hips and wet tongue on her breast made her scream again and again with ecstasy. The art of pleasuring a woman was one thing Ped' east had mastered. He was in control of the situation, and he knew from this night that he would be able to get anything he wanted.

Ped' east looked at the clock on the nightstand and realized that he had to hurry. He had the late show to do. A few extra twists and rotations of his hips and she released an exhausted shout of fulfillment. A few short seconds later, he erupted in blissful pleasure.

"You really know what you are doing, don't you?" Monet' said.

"I do my best" smiling, as he knew that he had been the ultimate satisfier.

"And you damn sure did that!" Monet' kissed his chest, let out a long sigh, and rolled out of bed. "What time do you have to be at the station?"

"In less than an hour."

"You're cutting it close, aren't you?

"Anything for you," Ped' east grinned slyly.

"Yeah, right." She smiled.

Ped' east jumped out of bed, smacked her on the ass, and walked past her to the shower. Ped' east felt like a champion fisher. Monet' took the bait as he reeled her in. He knew he had her in his hip pocket.

"Good evening, ladies and gentlemen. This is Paradise Soul Hour, and I am Ped' east, your host for the night. Bringing you urban music that lifts you higher and sets your ass on fire!"

Ped' east was getting his feel for the substitution thang. Although he worked for WRIA as a set producer, he knew that it would only be a matter of time before starting to be a regular on the air.

He was a hit at Grambling as a star DJ for the school radio station. He was affectionately known as the "trouble maker." At the present time, he was a substitute for Earl "Naughty Vibe" Phillips. Whenever Earl had something to do, he would get Ped' east to do the show. He knew that Ped' east was an "up and coming" producer and radio personality, and he felt like he was taking him under his wing with his gestures. Ped' east appreciated it because he genuinely respected Earl, and knew that he would learn a lot from him. Earl taught Ped' east all the "ins and outs'" of the business of New York radio. Ped' east also knew that sooner or later he would have to get out there on his own and make it all happen. Ped' east even understood the importance of connections and a ticket inside the world of stardom to have advantages for his clients. So, he held on to a life as a radio producer and a part-time gig producing young talent for the time being. Ped' east had the personality that could charm amazing talent to sign with his company. These two investments of his time would surely land him an opportunity to make it to the top, and that was what he was doing.

The show was a two-part show: One part slow, grooving R&B music and the other part call-ins about deep personal thoughts, questions, and comments from listening audiences. As the music started to die down, the mellow voice of Ped' east kicked in.

"This is Ped' east, what is your pleasure?"

"Hey, Ped' east. This is Marcy. I just wanted to say that I am glad that they are giving you a chance to be on the air. I think that your voice is so damn sexy!"

Ped' east could imagine the devilish grin on the other side of the line.

"Thank you, Marcy, I appreciate that. Let's hope that my bosses are listening in." Ped' east chuckled in a deep smooth voice.

"I'm for real. Your voice is like, Uh hmmm, diving into chocolate, and I like chocolate."

Ped' east began to blush but knew that he had to get her question underway and return to the music.

"Thanks again, so what is your question?"

"I just wanted to know why women seem to think they have to feel guilty and nasty after having had a great one nightstand. I mean, men don't feel the guilt, so why does society want us to feel we can be vibrant, consenting, sexual adults."

Ped' east knew that he had to give a smart answer. He knew that several hundreds of women would be listening, including the women who had something to do with his paycheck.

"Hey, I think that every woman is entitled to her own perception of herself. What others think should not outline who a woman is. You can only be destroyed mentally, emotionally, or physically when you allow yourself to be. No one can control what you think. If you are secure within yourself, you don't need validation from anyone. Be strong, sister, and to the rest of my Nubian queens out there; don't let the world define you. Put all the negativity behind you."

"Uhhmm, I like that answer. You really know how to make women feel good, don't you?" The caller said. Ped' east knew that he had hit a home run.

"I do my best," Ped' east said. "You have a good night, with your beautiful sounding voice."

"Good night," the caller said.

"This is Ped' east returning to the sounds, that help you calm down, but keeps your temperature rising." Ped' east put on the next track and started the next hour of music. He figured with a few more months in the industry, and a few more great answers to questions like tonight, in no time he would be a legend in New York. One of his colleagues tapped on the window and gave him the thumbs up. Ped' east smiled as he sat back in his chair.

Yeah, tonight was going to be a smooth night.

Kendall sat at the table full of bills. He didn't know how in the world he was going to pay all of these bills. Kendall knew calling home for money wasn't an option, because his father expected him to fail in the Big Apple. Kendall knew that something had to be done, but wasn't sure what to do. He had such good luck when he started his voyage in New York.

He landed two commercials that were running frequently and a temporary spot on a daytime soap opera. Kendall had a small apartment with all of the furnishings he needed to make it the perfect bachelor pad. He even bought himself a used car, although he used the subway most of the time because it was cheaper. Now the bills were coming in heavy, and the gigs were coming far and in-between. His rent was two months behind, and the creditors started calling about his car. The money he was making at the gym would not pay for the extravagant lifestyle that he tried to get when he first moved to New York. He knew now, he had made a premature decision, but it all happened so fast. Kendall was unaware of what he had gotten himself into. He thought about calling the pack, but he knew they all had bills of their own. Kendall walked toward the kitchen to pull a beer from the fridge, when he noticed the business card from Deacon, hanging out of his gym bag near the kitchen door. Deacon's proposition and the memory of the night before in the sauna room went through his head. Kendall pulled the card from the bag and contemplated calling his alluring associate. Kendall walked to the phone and started to dial the number but hung up before the second ring.

"I can't believe I am even thinking about this. This is so stupid. What am I thinking? I know that my parents would kill me. What would my big brothers think? Shit, they probably wouldn't care. Man, I need this money. I know that it would only be this one time. How hard could it be? I am an actor. I can do this. It is just another role, a script to learn, and money to collect." Kendall went on with these thoughts for what seemed hours.

In the end, had no other way to get himself out of this debt, and besides, he was a grown man, and the opportunity to please some women could not be that bad. Kendall picked up the phone and redialed the number. It was about 2:00 a.m., but Kendall was sure pimps didn't sleep. A slight grin came over him, although he was scared to death.

"Hello," Kendall heard Deacon mutter.

"Hey, Deacon, is that you?" Kendall's voice sounded much different than it did the night before.

"Yeah, who dis is?"

"This is Ken, from the gym. I know that it's late, and I may be disturbing you, but I have been thinking about your offer from the other day, and I want to take you up on it while I still have the nerve."

"Hey man, my offer is still on, I think you will be a great addition to my cast."

"Hey man, I will not be an addition, but rather a one-time wonder, depending on how much you are offering. By the way, how much are you offering?"

"Well, as you have been in several other things before, which means you have a little experience, how does five thousand grab you?"

"Five thousand dollars," Kendall tried to keep the excitement from showing in his voice. It was an attractive offer, and he desperately needed the money.

"Okay, Deac," Kendall said, "What are all of the stipulations?"

"Look, it is early in the morning, and we have a shooting tomorrow night, how about you meet me at my studio for 6:30? My address is on the card that I gave you. And I look forward to seeing you. I will give you all of the details then."

"A'ight, Deac, see you then." Kendall hung up the phone, but could not sleep. He went to the desk drawer and pulled out a pack of cigarettes he saved for moments when he couldn't quite think things through. So many thoughts ran across his mind that he knew sleep could not come for him tonight.

The subway was cold and crowded. The entire ride to the studio seems to take an eternity. Every moment Kendall thought about what he would have to do, ran through his mind a thousand times.

Man, I should just take my ass home and forget about this. Is my self-respect worth that much? I don't know what to do. Fuck it, I'm going home.

The subway doors opened, and Kendall was at the stop he needed to be. He guessed that it was his sign to go ahead and go through with it. Ken walked through the subway terminal and up into the cold streets of New York. He found the place he was looking for about a half a block from the subway station. It was a plain building, but I guess that was how studios like this one had to be, very inconspicuous. Kendall walked into the studio foyer and was greeted by a sexy woman with a thin frame and beautiful long, cold black flowing hair. Kendall felt calmer already.

"May I help you, sir" The receptionist smiled at him.

"Hello, my name was, is, uh hmm, Ken, Kendall Johnson."

"Kinda nervous, huh?" The woman's smile started to widen.

"This must be your first time?"

"Yes, it is," Kendall said.

"Don't be nervous, you are going to do just fine. Mr. Williamson is expecting you."

"Who" Kendall looked confused. "Deacon," he said. The lady giggled.

"Oh, yeah, Deacon."

Kendall's hands started to sweat. He knew that he couldn't turn back now. The lady led him into the studio; he saw several created scenes in the studio. Kendall continued to walk; he saw scene after scene of living rooms and bedrooms. He thought that he was about to be sick to his stomach. "Be strong!" He whispered to himself. Kendall was led into a room where he was greeted by Deacon, two other women, and an older thinning, gray-haired man. All of them had cameras.

"Oh, he is fine," the thin man said seductively.

Kendall looked strangely at the man as he reached to shake Deacon's hand.

"Hey, man, I see that you made it, and right on time." Deacon said.

"Yeah, I made it," Kendall said, trying to not show his nervousness.

"Well, I would love to talk with you, but we need to get some still shot pictures of you and get some screens done. All that I need to know is if you are ready?" Deacon said.

"Well, I guess that I am about as ready as I can be. Come on before I lose my nerve." Ken said.

"Okay, then, we need you to take off your clothes so we can get started."

Kendall started to unbutton his shirt but slightly paused when he realized that no one left the room. Kendall felt like he had to get control of himself, and knowing if he didn't, he would lose complete control of his position. He wanted to be the one in control, especially where his body was concerned. Kendall proceeded to take his shirt off. His head down as if to concentrate on his buttons, but he could feel the eyes attached to him. After Kendall removed the shirt from his chiseled body and removed his pants and underwear at the same time. He was scared but amazedly excited. Not only was he in great physical shape, but his penis was also a beautiful sight. He saw the eyes widen around him, and he knew that they liked what they saw. His penis, slightly stiff, and his mind still uneasy, Kendall looked up to find that they had already started to take snapshots of him. Deacon motioned for Kendall to follow him into the next room where they could really get started. The next place was a beanbag, a little pallet, and a Chinese folding divider for decoration. The ladies positioned Kendall across the pallet. He started to get more comfortable as they began to take more shots. His youthful body seemed to make love to the camera.

Kendall felt his penis awakening by every flash of the cameras around him. He was a natural. The uneasiness left, and he was the master of his fate. Then, a bald head, caramel-colored brother walked onto the set, fully nude, and sat beside Kendall on the mat. Kendall's smile left immediately but was unsure of the response that he was supposed to take. Then, another thin, dark-skinned brother, also nude, walked in and stood behind him. Kendall knew that he had been tricked.

"What the fuck is going on, Deacon? Who are these niggas?" Kendall wasn't about to hold his tongue.

"Calm down, man, I told you that it was an adult film." Deacon said in a low whisper.

"Yes, but what you didn't say was that I would be doing this flick with a bunch of faggots! You must have lost your damn mind, where the fuck are my clothes!"

"Come with me, man, into the room, let me talk to you."

"Hell no! All I want to do is to get my shit and get the fuck out of here!" Kendall was enraged.

Deacon led Kendall back into the room where his clothes were and shut the door behind them. Then, Deacon pushed the fear line.

"You stupid little punk!" Deacon looked at Kendall like he was an enemy waiting for the signal to kill. "Who the fuck do you think that you are coming into my establishment and disrespecting me! If you want to leave, then fine. But, what the fuck you got out there? You called me because you were broke, and bills are coming out of your ass left and right, remember? There are thousands of people who would love the type of money that I am offering you. You name me one other place that you can go to and make the kind of money that I am offering you." The anger in Kendall was still there but had slightly subsided. He had never seen this side of Deacon before. "And, that penny ass job at the gym cannot afford you the type of things that you want and need. So, what are you going to do? I thought that you were an actor. A great actor can play any type of role, whatever it is. If you can find something better, get dressed and walk your ass on out the way you came in!" Deacon had spoken his peace and was walking toward the door.

"Deac, man, hold on, this is just not me. I have never even remotely thought about anything like this in my life. I just don't think that I can do this." Kendall said, his voice barely above a whisper.

"It's acting man, that's all, it's a job, and it pays the bill, at least some of them." Deacon's voice seemed to calm down also. "Okay, can you give me five minutes to get myself together? Please." Deacon gave a faint nodding yes and walked out of the room. Kendall sat straddled across the folding chair. He didn't even notice the coolness of the chair on his naked bottom.

"Come on, Kendall, you can do this man, you are an actor. A great actor. But what was the pack gonna think? What will my family think? Man, you can't tell them this. Just get it over with and take yourself

home. I hope no one who I truly know and love would ever watch this video. But why would they watch an all-male movie?"

Kendall's stomach was in knots. He didn't know if he genuinely had a stomach attack or his nerves were eating away. Kendall looked down to see his penis had totally gone to sleep, which confirmed that he was not attracted to the guys he would encounter. He took a long breath and got up from the chair and started toward the door. One more deep breath and Kendall walked himself and his new character back onto the set.

"Deacon, I am an actor, and I am going to do my best to perform. This will be hard for me, but I chalk it up to experience." Kendall said.

Deacon nodded and gave Kendall a script. He took his place back on the pallet and read through the manuscript, and it was only a half a page of lines. The cameras began to roll, the scene started, and Kendall spat out his lines like a pro. When the lines were over, and the scene started, Kendall knew that the challenge was on. The men began to move across the floor onto the pallet. One of the men touched Kendall's knees as if to spread his legs. He hesitated for a moment and then let himself go. He closed his eyes and tried to imagine a woman licking his inner thighs. Tears formed in the corners of his eyes as the two men started to caress and fondle Kendall's body. Kendall's mind made his body play the part; his soul was punctured. He could hear the moans and smacks as they kissed each other and then Kendall. Kendall could feel the hot tongue of the men as they went down on him.

He knew that he shouldn't be here, but his manhood was still erect. Kendall tried his best to tune out the cameras and all of the people watching, taping, and staring in amazement. Ken felt violated like some prostitute in it for the money. Several scenes of his masculinity flashed before him; his little league days, hanging out with the fellas, dates, first love, college football, and fraternity days. Each memory seemed to fade with each second he spent in the twisted love scene. In the end, Kendall's body was drenched in sweat, spit, and semen. After the scene was over, the audience started clapping. Kendall got up, put on his clothes as fast as he could, and ran into the bathroom to throw up. He headed out of the door. He would get his check later.

Later that evening, Kendall stood in the shower for nearly an hour, cleaning every part of his body over and over again. He knew that he was crying, and the water from the shower was able to camouflage his external feelings. Still, the pain Kendall felt on the inside was more intense than he could imagine. How could he have kissed a man, let alone entered a man? Kendall started to cry louder. He had betrayed his manhood.

CHAPTER SEVEN

Ped' east unlocked the door of his apartment with a raised brow. Some of his things were different and could feel the awkwardness in the air. He walked into the den to find a sight that made the hair stand on his arm. It was Jessica, his first love and the only woman in this life that had ever held a part of his heart in her hands. It had been al8o8most six years since he had seen her. Jessica left college unexpectedly. Her parents didn't know where she was, and she did not return to Baton Rouge. Every relative was upset and worried. Only one of her girlfriends knew what happened to her, but she wouldn't say anything to Ped' east. All that she would say was, "Jessica is doing fine. Leave me alone and stop bothering her." She is gone, and she doesn't want to see you or anyone. Just know that she is okay; move on with your life!" Ped' east didn't know how to respond, but after time, he felt that all hope was gone and moved on, but his heart never did.

"What are you doing?" Ped' east said with a mixture of a smile and bewilderment.

"I had a little vacation time, and I wanted to come and see you." She smiled at him.

"Vacation from what, LIFE?! I have not heard from you in years, and you break in here and tell me that you had some vacation time, and you wanted to see me! You have a lot of damn nerve. I ought to call the police on your ass for breaking and entering. How did you even know where I live?"

"There are many things that you don't understand, and I want to talk with you about them. I just came to grips with all of the things that happened." Jessica said with a low tone. "Please, Peddy, I know that I didn't give you a chance, but will you give me one? I don't deserve it, but I surely need it."

Peddy! Ped' east had not heard that name in a very long time. It was the term of endearment that she gave him years ago. The girl could get anything out of him. She was the only girl who could pull his playa card. Even though he was tempted to put her ass out of his house, he knew that he had been waiting for this day for a very long time. Every night this moment crossed his mind, but he never expected it to happen. Black people don't believe in therapy, but Ped' east needed it. He felt that he would never be able to put this girl or their relationship behind him. Ped' east spent two years in therapy behind this woman. He was so depressed that some nights it was hard to breathe. He told his parents that it was because of school, but he did confess the truth to the therapist. This was his first love, and nothing he did or tried to do erased the memory of her. As his parents would say, she had his nose "wide open!" But inevitably, day by day, one step at a time, he came to grips with the notion that he might never see her again. Every other girl seems to be a ship passing in the Ped' east night, but Jessica had anchored into his dock for a very long time.

Jessica had a smile that could light up a room. Her soft, doe-like eyes with its light brown hue, straight white teeth that stood firmly behind two flawlessly full shaped lips, gave her the wonderful mixture of her African-American/Hispanic culture. And those lips were the kind of lips that kept a man hooked on her every word.

Her sandy brown hair hung gently, caressing her shoulders and stopping around her mid-back; it was the kind of hair a man could spend the entire day running his fingers through. She stood there in a classy low-cut dress that discreetly exposed her toned and taut body. She was the bomb, and Ped' east knew it. All of these years passed, and the vision he remembered in his mind about her was still the same. Jessica was all that.

"So, are you just gonna stand over there with your mouth open, drooling?" Jessica wasn't arrogant, but she didn't know how else to mask her nervousness other than the way Ped' east always known her.

"I guess you still think that you are all of that?" Ped' east tried to hold his composure as he walked toward her.

"No, it's not like that." Jessica played with the tip of her fingernail in her mouth, and she knew that drove Peddy crazy.

"How did you get in here, and how did you know where I was?"

"Don't worry about that. You know that I always get what I want, especially when a man is downstairs as the doorman. Also, I got in touch with your cousin Jermaine, and he told me."

"Jonathan let you into my apartment, and my big mouth ass cousin gave up the goods, huh?" Ped' east said with sharp anger.

"Come on, baby, don't be mad. You can't resist this, and neither could he."

"Look, I can't front and say that I am not surprised to see you. I can't say that I am not happy that you are alright, but you cannot walk back into my life after almost six years and pretend that everything is the way it was. I have grown up a lot since college. You put me through hell, and I won't let you do that to me again. I don't know what you expect to accomplish by this, but whatever it is you are selling, I ain't buying, not this time! Ped' east tried to sound really mad, but it started to sound rehearsed. These are all of the things he practiced for several years that he had been hoping to tell her but never had the chance. And now, his mouth was saying one thing, but his heart was telling another.

"I know that this is not easy for you, and it isn't for me either. I really need to be with you, but if you want me to walk away from here, I will. I know that I have no right to insist on anything, but I was hoping that you would help me." Jessica paused for a second, and when she heard no response, she turned to walk toward the door.

"Wait, bring your ass back here!" Ped' east didn't know why he was stopping her. This girl had left him high and dry years before, and now he was the one that had to play the forgiving role. What was the reason that she had come all of this way to see him?

What the hell, this excuse better be a good one. It wasn't like she was his wife, and he did have a great college life, so maybe he could make himself listen to whatever excuse she could possibly throw at him after all of these years. Then he would throw her out on her ass.

Whatever Jessica really had to talk about, she never did.

They sat on the living room floor and talked about past memories from Baton Rouge and GSU. Jessica always could work her magic on him, and she had not lost her touch after all these years. Although Ped' east wanted to be mad, it was surely a relief from the grind of life that confronted him daily.

"What the hell have you been doing with yourself all of these years?" Ped' east said anxiously.

"Well, I'm back in Baton Rouge. I lived with my parents for a couple of months, but I have my own place now. I have a job there. I was in Chicago, and I was able to finish my degree in mass communications. Still, after a while, Chicago was lonely and cold as a polar bear's pockets, and I knew that it was time for me to go home."

"Is that where you were all of those years? What possessed you to leave and go there? I really need some answers."

"Let's not talk about that right now. Trust me, I will tell you everything real soon."

How in the hell could this girl still have these effects on me after all of these years? This was crazy! It was surely a bittersweet night.

D.J. heard some noteworthy people were supposed to be at the club tonight. Zodana, Tommy Phillipe', and Jai-Waye were supposed to be headlining at the Singer Theater. It was rumored they would be at the club to chill after the concert. D.J. had been in New York for the past two and a half years, and he was very proud of the breaks he had gotten since moving to the Big Apple. Still, he was awaiting the moment he would be headlining notable concert halls. What if they came into the club tonight and heard him sing? D.J. had a name at the club. People from all parts of New York were coming to the club to listen to him sing. As he had been at the club, the manager took a chance on him and allowed him to use his own material; so for the last year, D.J. had been singing the music he composed.

As the daylight began to fade, D.J. rode the subway over to the club. He genuinely enjoyed going to work. Dexton promised himself that he would do everything possible to make a life for himself as a singer. He pulled the skullcap tightly down on his ears as he began his two-mile walk to the club, quietly sing a tune. The cold air made the words seem to appear before his eyes in a foggy image. He had a good feeling about tonight. As he entered the club, the chairs were still neatly placed on the tables.

"Hey, Nico, why haven't y'all started opening the club? You know some 'big-wigs' may be here tonight." D.J. said, wondering what was going on.

"Man, Sekou is not coming in tonight. You know his dumb ass is not dependable. I'm about to fire his trifling ass." D.J. smiled. Nico seemed really pissed.

Nico was an old playa. You could always depend on him to make you laugh. He was the type who wore bold colors like spring green and orange. Nico had nine children by six different women. He was definitely an old "O.G." "No problem, Nico, I will help you get everything straight."

"Cool! Paule' and Mikiel will be in within the next hour, so I think we will be ready for opening." Nico said to D.J.

It was now 9:45, and the club was packed. The band was setting the mood, and the people were laughing, dancing, and drinking. Nico loved that. This meant that people would be buying drinks and making his pockets larger. It was almost time for D.J. to do his second set when the pack walked in. They were not famous people that he was looking for, but it was always a pleasure to see them.

"What's up, dog?" Ped' east said. D.J. grinned widely and walked toward his brothers.

"What are y'all doing here?" D.J. said.

"Big brother, I have some great news for you. I got a call from Joya Reynolds's agents. They want me in her next video and a backup dancer for her concert tour starting in a couple of months." Trip waited for the expression on his brother's face that gave him the approval he needed.

"Alright, little brother! I am so proud of you, man." D.J. picked his brother up in a big bear hug.

"Come on, man, put me down. We are in public!" Trip playfully said to his brother.

"Come on, punks, I have a rep to protect. I can't be seen with no floaters," Ped' east said.

"You know what you can do with that floating bullshit!" Trip said.

"Do you ever watch your mouth?" D.J. spoke with a raised brow.

"Hell, no!" Trip said, trying to make his brother mad. Damn, they got some freaks in here!" Trip said, wiping his mouth, pretending that he was salivating.

"You are so stupid!" D.J. said, trying to ignore his brother. "Hey, where is Kendall?" D.J. said, looking in wonder.

"Man, we called him two thousand times, but we got no answer. I just left a message on his answering machine. I told him where we were going to be and to meet us." Ped' east said.

D.J. showed his brothers to the VIP area. He fellas went on chatting and drinking and vibing to the music. A loud outburst of laughter came from the small table. To the fellas, the rest of the club didn't exist.

"Come on, man, we are too loud," D.J. said.

"Fuck 'em," Trip giggled loudly and slightly inebriated.

"D.J., now you know how we gon' act when we get together, especially when we get a Lil' fire in our system." Ped' east said.

D.J. was about to comment when he caught a glimpse that made his heart almost stop. Heading toward the VIP area was Zodana, Tommy Phillipe' and Jai-Way.

"Oh, Shit!" Trip said, almost falling out of his seat.

"Man, do you know who that is?" Trip said in a loud voice.

"Yeah, fool, stop being a damn teenaged groupie. Have some class!" Ped' east said obviously feeling the alcohol too.

Nico led them to the table himself. He walked with his chest poked out because the big-name celebrities came into his establishment.

"D.J., let me introduce you to Ms. Zodana, Mr. Tommy Phillpe' and Jai-Waye.

"It is very nice to meet all of you." D.J. mouthed, obviously intrigued by the guests.

Trip tugged at his pants leg, and D.J. gave him a quick, swift kick. "Awe punk!" Trip frowned, not caring who was around.

"This is my upcoming talent!" Nico smilingly said the guest, something that he had never done before. "He'll be in rare form in just a few minutes."

D.J. was not used to the praise that Nico was throwing his way. He wasn't sure if it was genuine or was just doing a plug for his club's atmosphere. The guest took their seats next to the pack, and Nico left with a jackal smile across his face. The waitress came to take the drink orders. The guests seemed to cool within the soul groove of the band.

D.J. took the stage. He felt a chill past through him. This breeze is one that was felt every day for the past six months. D.J. felt that his parents always showed up to give him encouragement every time he needed them. He knew that he would need them tonight. Even though he sang on this very stage night after night for the past two years, it was different with celebrities in the audience. The band started playing, and Trip jumped up, half-drunk before D.J. even sang a word.

"That's my big brother!" D.J. looked in amazement. He motioned for Ped' east to sit Trip down.

"Come on, man, don't embarrass your brother." Ped' east said.

D.J. took a quick glance over the audience and a deep breath and started to do what he did best.

"The view from the top is what you are aiming for. Even though the struggle is in the climb, it makes you appreciate the view from the top. I have struggled for years to find you, girl, you are my vision from the top, and the view looks good from up here, girl."

D.J. felt his comfort zone and began to play with the audience through his eyes. And then his focus fell on Zodana. She seemed to really be vibing.

"I wish that others could see my reality. I wish that others only knew the encouragement I have from this magnificent view, and the view is you girl. D.J. had the audience in the palm of his hands."

Celebrities or not, no one could resist the sweet voice of Dexton "D.J." Cummings. When D.J. finished the song, he found himself on his knees and the audience giving him a standing ovation. Of course, Trip was jumping and screaming to the top of his lungs about how D.J. was his brother. D.J. kissed two of his fingers, placed them across his heart, lifted them into the air, gave honor to God, and recognized his deceased parents.

The rest of the night seemed a breeze. Each song seemed better than the first. During the last song, he saw the guest get up and leave. As he sang, his eyes followed them to the back and out of doors. D.J. wished that he could have said goodbye to them, but it was too late. D.J. finished the set and went to join his brothers at the table.

"It's getting late, man, we are about to leave." Ped' east said.

"Yeah, I am tired too, big brother. We are about to fly." Trip spoke very low. He was wasted, and he needed some sleep, although some strong coffee would have worked better.

"Alright, dudes, peace out. Trip, I will see you at home." D.J. said.

The brothers put their index fingers together as they always did in parting, Ped' east, and Trip walked out of the club. D.J. sat down to breathe for a moment. Mikiel walked up to him and handed him a note. And, it read:

Hello Dexton,

I really enjoyed listening to you sing. You really got skills. I love the original music that you gave us. You really have talent. If you can, I would love for you to come to the concert tomorrow. If you can come, call this number (555) 436-6128. I will set up backstage passes for you. I hope that you can make it.

- Zodana.

D.J. could not believe his eyes. He read the note three times before he jumped from the chair. "Oh my God, Zodana, wants to see me! Oh my God," D.J. ran straight to the phone in the back hall of the club. He had to call the pack. He dialed Kendall's number because he knew neither Trip nor Ped' east had gotten home yet. He was so excited he could have exploded. The phone rang, but there was no answer. This was strange, no one heard from Kendall. The answering machine picked up and D.J. message:

"Dawg, you are not gonna believe this man, Zodana was at the club tonight, and she heard me sing. She even left me a note talking about how she liked my show. She wants me to come to her concert tomorrow with backstage passes. Isn't that shit the bomb? Okay, get at me, dawg. I am waiting to hear from you."

D.J. hung up the phone totally elated by the night that magically spun before him.

Kendall sat in his bathrobe in front of the television. He was unshaven and roughly dirty. It had been two weeks since he had done the video, but events of his actions replayed in his mind every second of every hour. Kendall had not been to the gym since the taping of the movie. He heard all of the messages that each person left him, but he neither did have the strength or the courage to pick up the phone nor the mental stability to talk with anyone. He vaguely smiled as he heard the message from D.J., but knew that he just could not speak with him. Ped' east and Trip had even come by the house, but Kendall looked through the peephole, saw who it was, and quietly stole back into his bedroom's security. He was just not ready to face his brothers. Not now, maybe not ever again. That dreaded day made his perception cloudy. His tears of emotion seemed to overflow like an irregular dripping faucet that would never turn off, no matter how hard you turned the fixture.

Kendall pulled himself up from the couch and into the kitchen. He needed the Pepto-Bismol from the cabinet. His stomach was weak and queasy. He hadn't eaten much, but his stomach seemed to always rumble. In the top cabinet, Kendall reached for the Pepto when the Tylenol fell and spilled onto the floor. Kendall reached down, on his hands and knees, to pick up the aspirin, and a crazy thought entered his mind. "Why don't you just go ahead and take your life. You are scared now; you will never again have a normal life. You stupid punk, you have disrespected your family, your friends, and especially yourself. Go ahead and kill yourself. You are walking dead anyway!" Kendall sat on the floor as the tears started to flow again. He wanted to be a stronger man and to stop the crying, but he couldn't.

He wanted to forget the past and begin again, but he couldn't, and there was no one that he knew of that could help him through this. In despair, Kendall looked at the twelve pills that he was holding in his hands. Maybe he could get rid of the pain by just getting away. Perhaps he could save his family, friends, and himself from the shame by just taking his life. He didn't need to leave a note of any sort, and so no one would know what the real problem was. Kendall put the pills into his mouth with watery eyes, but suddenly the doorbell rang, and Kendall snapped out of his deadly trance and spit the pills onto the floor. The doorbell rang a third time before Kendall got up from the floor, wiped his eyes, and headed toward the door. Through the peephole, Kendall saw Jason. He wiped his eyes once again, tied the robe tighter, and opened the door. It was too late to clean up, and he really could have cared less.

Kendall wanted to again steal away into his room, but he feared that if he didn't talk to someone, the next time he would succeed in his little suicide episode. He had nothing to lose by talking to Jason, although it would be rough talking to anyone. Reluctantly, he opened the door.

"What is up, man? I left you several messages, and no one has heard from you. You have not been into work in two weeks, and I was worried about you bruh." Jason said, noticing the redness of Kendall's eyes. Kendall did not respond. "What is wrong man, are you trying to drop off the face of the planet?"

"Hey, man, I appreciate your concern, but I really cannot talk with you now. Can you come back?" He really didn't want him to leave, but he couldn't let on that easily that he desperately needed to talk to someone because he was lost and didn't know how to find his way back.

Jason noticed the brush off, and Kendall was not going to get off that easy.

"Come on, man, you don't stay anywhere remotely close to me. It took me a minute to get it out of our boss to tell me where you lived. I came all of this way to check on you, and you give a brotha the cold shoulder. We have been boys for some time now. I know that something is wrong with you. You look like shit!"

Kendall walked back into the apartment and sat down on the couch. Jason closed the door behind himself and followed Kendall into the living room area and sat down in the chair nearest the sofa.

"Come on, man, don't leave me hanging. Whatever it is that has gotten you in this state has got to be bad, and I don't think that you should go through it alone." Jason said, rubbing his hands together in anticipation of Kendall's news.

"You wouldn't understand, no one would," Kendall said, trying to fight back the tears.

"How will you know that if you don't trust me?" Jason said, pulling the chair to Kendall on the couch. "Come, one man, you need me, and I am your friend," Jason spoke in a tone that let Kendall know that he was listening and concerned.

Kendall looked into Jason's eyes and knew that he was telling the truth. He had to get rid of some of the pain that he was feeling, so he let himself go and proceeded to tell Jason the whole story with all of its embarrassing details. At the end of the lengthy story, Kendall was in full tears. He just knew that Jason was about to laugh or walk out in disgust, but that was not what he did. Jason got up from his chair and sat on the couch close to Kendall and gave him a manly hug. Kendall let go of every tear that was in him, which seemed to last several minutes. After Kendall seemed to calm down, Jason spoke warmly to him.

"My brother, you did what you had to do. You don't have anything to be ashamed of. People live their entire lives in shame and doubt, worrying about things that they cannot change in the past. You are a good man, and you don't have anything that you need to be ashamed of. Screw the world man, and live for yourself." Jason's words were comforting to him. Outside of the pack, Kendall didn't know of anyone that would give him such good advice, and he was glad that Jason had stopped by. He didn't feel one hundred percent better, but anything was better than the way he was feeling.

"Get up, man, go take a shower, shave, and let's go get lunch." Kendall didn't really feel like eating, but he did need to get out of the house. Jason turn on the T.V., got comfortable on the couch, and Kendall left the room, and walked into the back to get ready. Kendall found a new true friend, and it felt good.

"Let me run you some bath water and fix you something to eat. I know that you have had a long day." Jessica said as Ped' east walked into the house.

Ped' east thought that he was dreaming. He should have been pissed; hell, he should have been totally outraged. In his mind, every scene was playing itself out, but everything seemed to be moving in slow motion. Why did he continue to let the "torture of his past" continue her games? "Jessica, you don't have to do that."

"I know that I don't, but I want to." Ped' east wanted to be stronger, but he just wasn't. Damn! Of all of the women he banged and left behind, this was just one woman that held him under her spell.

"Now you go into the bathroom and take a warm bath, I ran you some water. Let me start cooking, and I will be in there in a moment to wash your back."

"Ped' east, although confused, excited, anxious and curious, did as she said and walked toward the bathroom. As he walked in, he could feel the warmth of his Jacuzzi and cold smell his masculine soothers lightly filled the air. He smiled, knowing that it was moments like these, which set his sour afire. He stepped out of his clothes into the hot, steaming, bubbling waters of the Jacuzzi. The rose petals were a nice touch. Ped' east did not mind at all being pampered by a woman. As he sank into the water, Ped' east could hear Jessica humming from the kitchen. His mind began to steal back to the times that she was the only thing that he lived for. Jessica was the one that made him serious about going into the producing and radio industry. His thoughts continued to linger back over the pleasurable moments that they had spent together.

The first time they made love was way back out on his grandfather's farm. They took a long walk along the trail that led directly into the woods. The woods that Ped' east had spent many a quiet time in, alone, just and his thoughts. In the deepness of the woods was a small field that he discovered. In this field grew high grass, beautiful wildflowers, and one large oak tree that would welcome a light breeze. I was like something out of a magical picture book. Ped' east used to sit out there for hours at a time. He would wonder about life, his future, crying away his sorrows, telling the wind his secrets, and praying to God when things got too hard to handle. Ped' east brought Jessica to his secluded hideaway. A place that he had never taken anyone, not even the pack. This is the reason that he knew that he loved Jessica. As they lay on a blanket in the field, it started to rain. The sun was still shining, and the steady pour of the rain began. Ped' east's heart started to beat faster. It was the perfect moment to make love and be at one with nature. He gave her body pleasures that he didn't even think was possible. The mixture of the rain, passion, privacy, risk of being caught, and love between them was like reading from a romance novel.

Ped' east flashed back to reality, he found his penis hard, and his hand gently rubbed himself. This would be the perfect moment to enjoy an exciting moment of masturbation, but he decided against it. He was hoping that Jessica would grant him the opportunity of making love to her not long from now.

"Damn boy, you don't want to do anything that you are going to regret. I know that you want me to set you free, but I have plans for you a little later on. Now be good!" Ped' east was pointing to his penis in chastisement.

He finished his bath, got out of the tub, rubbed his smooth skin with cocoa-butter, wrapped himself in his silk bathrobe, checked out his hair and face in the mirror, and proceeded to walk out of the bathroom. Jessica was supposed to wash his back, but he figured that she would just owe him later, and he would use that playa's card if he needed to.

As he made his way to the kitchen, he noticed the living room floor was set. There was a fuzzy blanket lying on the floor. The fireplace was lit, and the crackle of the fire was quietly pleasant. Jazz playing in the background, and it seemed to set a tone of class and elegance. Two places had been set on the floor, with wine glasses, plates, candles, silverware, and some of the best smelling food Ped' east had inhaled in a long time. She made seafood gumbo with all the southern ingredients and spices. This savory aroma gave him a tinge of nostalgia that brought him back to Louisiana.

It reminded him of the time where he and Jessica had shared a picnic in their secret spot.

"Come on, baby. I know that you are hungry." She winked at him.

"What is that smell? It's goin' on up in here."

"Just a little southern cooking. I know that you have not had any in a while, and I just wanted to bring a little bit of food in your mouth.

"Mmmmmmmmmmm, mmm! This is good." Ped' east could not hide the pleasure this entire night was bringing him. He expected to come home, flop across the couch, and eat some cold, leftover pizza and drink a beer while trying to find something on the T.V. This is a ritual he did nightly when he was not hanging out with the pack.

Jessica grabbed his hand and led him to the place she had set. Damn. He noticed that booty, and he smirked, thinking that his slightly hairy friend might just get what it wanted. The next hour would be spent reminiscing over the pleasures of the past. He couldn't believe how good this food was. Every spice reminded him of why Louisiana was famous for exciting the taste buds, and so many people traveled there for that reason.

Jessica was the perfect conversationalist as she always was. He could never win an argument with her once she started to flash that beautiful smile. The room was just perfect for intimate conversation and light-hearted pleasantries. The food was great, the company was even better, and the night was perfect.

"I enjoyed that!" Ped' east said as he picked his teeth and let out a hearty belch while patting his stomach.

"Ewww, that's nasty," Jessica said jokingly. "Oh, don't get too full, you have not tried my strawberry shortcake." She got up from the floor and walked swiftly into the kitchen and came back with the cake. Jessica cut him a piece, put it on a plate, and placed it in front of him. Ped' east gave a sly grin and took some of the whipped cream and placed it in his mouth.

"What is wrong with you?" Jessica said.

"Nothing."

"What's going on in that head of yours?"

Ped' east eased his way to Jessica with a look of lust in his eyes. As his emotions flooded back, he grabbed the side of her face, looked into her eyes, and began kissing her neck. He paused for a moment to see what kind of response he was getting from her. Her eyes were closed, and he knew that it was on! His familiar sixth sense with women suddenly kicked in. He reached for the cake and scooped up a large portion of the cream with his fingers and put his fingers in her mouth. She moaned and moved to get a more comfortable position on the floor slightly under his body. Ped' east licked her neck, leaving traces of whipped cream. He licked up her neck and bit gently, where he knew she enjoyed it. Her moans started to intensify, and it drove his penis insane. He pulled her on top of him and rubbed his penis against her clitoris, slowly.

The pleasure of this foreplay set off electric sensations throughout her body. Jessica was a loud lover, and Ped' east loved it.

"Fuck!" She exclaimed as she grabbed it. She had to hold it in her hands to bring back the feeling she had missed for so long ago. He got harder in her hands, and she could feel its pulsation every second that she held it. The girth of it in her hands told her that she had to have it deep within her. He kissed her shoulders as he pulled the straps of her dress down her arms. She wasn't wearing a bra, and her nipples seemed to break the threads of the dress as they protruded against it. Ped' east once again kissed her neck, and then he gently nibbled her breast while they were still in the dress.

"Oh shit, that feels soooo fucking good!" Jessica yelled out in pleasure.

He continued to tug at the dress until her breasts were exposed. He then proceeded to tease her by licking around her nipples while cupping her breast in his hands. Jessica threw her head back as she combed through his hair. Ped' east knew Jessica couldn't handle the teasing any longer as he engulfed her nipples in his mouth. He bit down on her nipple, and she moaned with a mixture of pain and pleasure. As he continued to nibble on her breasts, he slipped two fingers into her already-wet vagina. Jessica began riding his fingers, which gave him permission to have his way with her.

"Damn, I missed your dick, Daddy. Fuck me!"

Ped' east grinned. As he started to move his fingers in rhythm, Jessica's moans heightened, and her hips seemed to meet every thrust from his thick fingers. The sounds exuding from her lips sent precum oozing from his throbbing penis. He removed his glistening fingers from within her and placed them hungrily into his mouth. He grinned devilishly and kissed her passionately. He then kissed down her neck and then cleavage until he was licking her inner naval. Her body was ready for whatever. Her voice sang filthy words, which made his penis expand with every sound. Ped' east knew that it was time. With that in mind, he slipped his mouth between her legs and ignited the volcano inside her. Her body twitched in excitement from the sensation of his tongue and mustache. Jessica crossed her legs around the back of his neck, forcing his tongue to go deeper inside her. She hadn't felt a tongue like that in a long time, and Ped' east was the only one that could make her feel this way. "Oh my God, this feels sooooo fucking good!" Jessica said as she gripped his hair. The slurping sounds he produced from between her legs spoke volumes, and the circular motions he created with his tongue had her floating to the heavens. Before she allowed her climax to approach, she stopped him abruptly.

It was now his turn to become the feast she had been yearning for. She kissed him slowly, yet purposefully letting him explore her body. Jessica pushed him backward, ripped open his bathrobe, and began to nibble very intensely on his nipple. He clutched the couch and bit his lip hard. Jessica then eased her way down, caressing his chest in the process until she came in contact with his penis. Her mouth watered at his big penis. When she held his penis in her hands, she looked up at Ped' east, letting him know what was next. She took him into her mouth, going slowly. Before he knew it, she made a vacuum of her throat and sped up, sending chills through his body. Ped' east grabbed Jessica's head aggressively, yet passionately forced him deeper into her warm, slippery mouth. Then it happened, Ped' east let out a scream that would be heard through the walls. He fully exploded into her mouth as his toes began to curl, and she swallowed every drop.

"Ohhhhhhh, Ohhhhhh," Ped' east exclaimed.

Ped' east struggled to control himself. Although he was enjoying the treatment, he was ready to make Jessica scream his name. Ped' east picked her up from the floor and tossed her on the couch. With both his hands tightly holding her waist and legs sitting high on his shoulders, he entered her body as the sweat fell off his chest onto her breast. No longer was Ped' east a quiet lover. Fuck the neighbors, he waited too long for this a moment, and he was going to enjoy it. He wanted her to feel every hard muscle that belonged to him, especially the one between his legs. Jessica let out a screech that let Ped' east know her orgasm was quickly approaching.

This excited him to uncontrollable pleasure. He penetrated Jessica deeply and swiftly. As he thrust in and out as the room became hot and humid. He was breathing on her neck, and with long strokes, he pleased her, and she scratched his back and held on for dear life. He picked her up and turned them around so that she was on top. He slipped into her and tapped her thigh, which let her know it was her time to shine. She moved her hair out of her face and began riding him slowly. He gripped her ass firmly and grunted at her, moving up and down on his shaft. After he had enough, he looped his arms under her legs and into her deeply.

"Fuck," she said as her eyes rolled into the back of her head and she moaned loudly. The juices dripped down both of their legs as their climax approached. Surprisingly, they climaxed at the same time. They panted while riding out their orgasm. Exhausted and satisfied, Ped' east laid on the side of her.

"Damn! You still got it," Jessica said.

Ped' east smiled at her as he pulled her up for one last kiss. He held her in his arms and never wanted to let her go. This was a feeling that he had been missing, and no other woman could do to him what she did so naturally. He knew she would not be staying long, but wished that she could. Oh, well, he would at least enjoy the rest of the night. He picked her up off the couch and into the soft comfort of his bed. Nothing was better to send him into a dream world than making love to the one woman he would give.

CHAPTER EIGHT

· · · · · · ●●● ● ●●● · · · · · ·

Trip was exhausted from the rehearsal. Joya Reynolds was not there, but rehearsals still had to go on. He sat in the corner with the rest of the dancers. It was about 2:45 p.m., and they had been going since 9:30 a.m. Show business was hard work, but he loved it. They sat around and talked about stupid things, and of course, Trip was the center of attention. His quick wit, bright smile, and beautiful green eyes were enough to keep the crowd's attention. The rehearsal went on about another hour with a lunch break, only a ten-minute break every now and then. After a very strenuous rehearsal, it was time for everyone to break for dinner. Heading out the door, the producer and a man stopped Trip and asked to see him in his office. Trip looked strangely. He was always in trouble, but he knew that he had not done anything this time. He reluctantly followed the producer and the other gentlemen into the producer's office.

"Marcus, I want to introduce you to Mr. Thomas Pikes. Mr. Pikes, this is Marcus Cummings." The producer said.

"Please, call me Trip."

"Okay, Trip, how are you?"

"Fine, sir." Trip said.

"I will leave you two alone, I know that there are some things that you want to talk with Trip about," said the producer. The producer walked out of the office, and Trip waited silently to hear what the man wanted. His heart was beating fast. His mind kept going over what he did or could have done.

"Mr. Cummings, Trip, I work for a modeling agency, and we are looking for some new, fresh faces to head up our new hip-hop clothing line. Right now, we are the third-largest urban wear company running at a close margin behind Sean John and South Pole. The name of our new line is *SemajE*, and I think that you have a look that will sell it." Mr. Pikes looked wondering if Trip was buying what he was selling. "I can promise you that if you let me, I will make you a star." Trip listened to everything that Mr. Pikes had to say. He could not believe what he was hearing. Was this man offering him a modeling deal?

"So, are you saying that I will be modeling?" Trip said, trying to contain his excitement.

"Sir, you will be plastered all over this city, the state, and the world. With your build and this exotic look, I know that you will go straight to the top and be a household name."

Trip started jumping up and down, shaking the man's hand. It was too late for any sort of tack. Trip was overwhelmed with the gesture, and that was a feeling that he could not hide.

"Hold on, Mr. Cummings, there will be a couple of screen tests and samples that we have to do, but I think that you are going to be perfect for the job. Here is my card. Do you think you can meet with my partners and me next Wednesday to go over the sample tests, contract, agreements, etc.?" Mr. Pikes said, very politely.

"Sure thing, thank you very much" Trip flashed that winning smile that he knew was one of the most important reasons that he was offered the job.

Ped' east finally made it through the traffic to Kendall's house. He left several messages, but Kendall had not returned them. It was a Saturday morning, and he had time off to get over to Kendall's house to see why he had not been in touch. Although the pack did not see each other that often, at least when they left messages, they would call each other back. After climbing three flights, Ped' east was out of breath. He knew that he needed to get back into the gym. Ped' east knocked on the door. Jason answered the door holding a basketball.

"Who are you?" Ped' east asked.

"I am Jason, I work at the gym with Kendall."

"Is he here?" Ped' east said.

"Yeah, he's here, but he is in the shower. We just got back from shooting some hoops. And you are?" Jason said.

"I am Ped' east."

"Oh, you are one of the pack. Kendall talks about y'all all the time. Nice to meet you, man."

"Likewise!"

Ped' east entered the apartment and walked into the back where Kendall was. Jason closed the door and went back into the living room and finished watching the football game. Ped' east walked straight into the bathroom without knocking.

"Where the hell have you been and why have you not been in touch with us?" Ped' east asked.

"Yo, Ped' east, man, what's up?" Kendall yelled from behind the shower curtain.

"Don't change the subject man, where have you been?"

"I was out of town. I went to Baton Rouge to take care of some business for my father. I told y'all that I would be gone for a week or so." Kendall lied carefully. He didn't want any of the pack to know what he had gone through.

"Hell no, you didn't, we would have remembered that." Ped' east belted out angrily.

"Man, my bad, I really thought that I told y'all I would be leaving for a minute," Kendall said, turning off the water and getting out of the shower.

"Anyway, you had us worried sick. We have been calling your ass for the longest. We called you from the club. Do you know that D.J. sang for Zodana, Tommy Phillipe', and Jai-Waye? Man, can you imagine the night that we had? And, your black ass missed it." Kendall felt that Ped' east was starting to calm down.

"Hey, you met Jason?"

"Yeah, he seems cool."

"Yeah, he works at the gym with me. We just got back from hooping, and I whooped him, but man, I am getting old. I never sweated so much in all of my life."

"You crazy, dude."

"Are you gonna be on the air tonight, man?"

"Yeah, I will be on there tonight. I am not sure what is going on at the studio, but the regular may be leaving. I think for a better deal somewhere else, and that may leave me in the right place at the right time."

Ped' east loved talking about the possibilities of moving to new levels in the industry. He was constant in making his dreams come true. Kendall finished dressing and was headed toward the kitchen.

"Man, I think that I have the worst gas problem of all. I haven't even eaten, and my stomach is aching. Kendall reached into the cabinet, pulled a bottle of Pepto, and took a two-spoon swig. "Ahhh, Pepto always hits the spot!" Kendall said.

"Alright, I need to get back on my side of town and get to the station to pay bills."

"Cool, I'll holla at you," Kendall said.

The two guys raised their fingers together as they always did.

"Nice meeting you, Jason." Ped' east said.

"Likewise," said Jason.

Ped' east walked into his apartment. He had about two hours before he was due at the station. Maybe he and Jessica could slip in a quickie before getting to work. It's been good having her in his life again. They broke up when they decided to go to different colleges, but they would remain special friends. Ped' east knew that whenever it was time to settle down, she would be the one.

"Jessica? I'm home, honey!" He called. "Sweetheart, are you here?"

Ped' east placed his keys on the key holder attached to the wall and walked further into the apartment. He called for her again, and she didn't answer. He checked the bedroom, and there was no sign of her or any of her belongings. Ped' east then walked into the kitchen. There he saw a note on the table.

Peddy,

I guess you know by now that I am gone. I had a wonderful time with you. I hope you feel the same. You are really the only one who can make me feel special. I wish I could stay longer, but I really have to leave. The job is calling. I never got a chance to say to you what I really needed to say, but I was really enjoying myself. You have treated me like a queen. I didn't want all of the drama, I know that it would be hard for me to say goodbye, so I guess this is the best way to do this. I will call you later. Thank you for being such a sweetheart.

Jessica

Ped' east let out a sigh and knew that the vacation was over. This was a woman who seemed to once again steal his heart. Damn! The house was empty again. He had been in this house a thousand times by himself, but this was the first time he felt alone. He walked over to the refrigerator and got himself a beer. How could he let her do this to him again? This time he didn't feel cheated; he just felt empty. He walked into the living room to start watching T.V. He still had about an hour before his long ride at the station began, and he chose to rest for a moment with thoughts of Jessica. Why the hell did she walk back into his life?

"D.J., what's up, man?" Ped' east said with a lowness in his voice.

"Nothing, man. Just hanging around the house, pretending that I am cleaning. You know how real bachelors do it." D.J. said with a slight chuckle. "What is up with you?"

"Man, I need to ask your advice on something."

"Shoot, my brother, I'm listening."

"Man, Jessica has left, and I don't know what to do. I thought that I would be alright when she left, but I am feeling really strange.

"Did you tell her about your feelings before she left?"

"Man, she knew. I tried my best to make sure that she knew."

"Hello, did you tell her how you felt?" The tone in D.J.'s voice started to change.

"Man, that girl knows that I am digging on her. Why a nigga gotta go through all of that drama to make a broad believe?"

"Listen to you, man. You are not a kid. Stop trying to be something that you are not. You know how to express yourself, and if Jessica is the woman who you want to be with, I say, go for it."

"I don't know how to start. You know D.J., when I am on the radio, it is like I am someone else. I can invent my character. Even when I am making love to a woman, I know what to do because I have been in the game for a long time, but I just can't make my mind and my heart connect long enough to make my mouth say the right things."

D.J. started to laugh. "Damn, that was profound! You should write a love novel."

"Fuck you, dude!"

"Okay, okay, I'm sorry."

"Come on, man. I see now that I can't talk with ya ass about Nothing."

"A'ight, I said that I was sorry. But look, I think that if you are that serious, you need to see her. Maybe y'all have some things that need to be discussed. Hey, you are not too young to be in love, and you have to be real with yourself first and foremost, and if love is what it is, admit to it and do something about it."

"I hear ya, man. I will get back with you in a couple of days. I have some "thangs" that I need to do. It's time for a vacation.

"Okay, dawg, keep me posted."

"You know that I will, my brother. Thank you for all of your help."

"Anytime!" D.J. got off the phone feeling really good about what he had told his friend, his brother.

Ped' east packed a small bag, called the radio station to tell them that he would not be there for a couple of days, and boarded the plane. This was the first time that he had gone after Jessica. He was going to tell Jessica exactly how he felt. He knew that he could not lose her again.

Ped' east could not believe what he was about to do. He has never done anything this crazy before in his life. He didn't know if he would even have the courage to go through with it once he made it to Baton Rouge. Whizzing through the clouds allowed him to go over what the hell he was going to say to Jessica. Ped' east didn't know if he wanted marriage or anything like that, but he knew that he loved her and that maybe one of the only means that allowed him to be with her. He didn't know, he just wanted Jessica.

CHAPTER NINE

• • • • • • • • ● • • • • • • • • •

D.J. arrived home from his morning jog and checking his mailbox. As he entered the apartment, he saw the blinking light on his answering machine. He pushed the button to hear his messages and sat at the table to sort through the mail. D.J. could not believe the voice that was on his machine.

"Hello, Dexton, this is Zodana, Zodana Ryan. I hope that you remember me." Yeah, right girl, how could I forget Zodana Ryan, D.J. thought to himself. "I know that this is strange for me to be calling you. I was wondering if you were still coming to the show tonight." D.J. was jumping up and down like a kid who heard the ice cream man's truck coming from around the corner. "I know that this is probably bothersome, but I thought that I would give it a try. If you can't come, I understand, but I really would like to see you." D.J. almost fainted. He immediately called the pack to let them listen to the message. He knew that he would never erase that message from his machine. In fact, it would be something that he would let everyone who came to his home listening to it.

D.J. walked through the mall by himself. He had to find the right outfit to wear to the concert tonight. He knew he should have brought one of the boys with him, but he couldn't wait; it was a spur of the moment. D.J. walked from store to store, trying to find something special to wear and didn't see what he was looking for. "You'd think that with all of these stores in this huge mall, you would be able to go to any store and find something to wear," D.J. said to

84

himself. D.J. walked into the next department store. It must have been a newly opened store because D.J. had not seen it before. "BC Chay's" was the name. It seemed to be a combination of urban hip-hop and conservative casual. D.J. didn't know if he would like the store, but he proceeded on into it. A pretty young girl with dimples that you could see even when she wasn't smiling, greeted him. Her hair was braided back in straight-shoulder length cornrows. D.J. thought that she was cute.

"Can I help you?" the young lady said.

D.J. then saw a sight that really blew his mind. Her entire set of top teeth was covered with gold. "Man, how can a woman this fine have all of those gold teeth?" D.J. thought. Then D.J. noticed that name that she had tattooed into her neck. D.J. sighed quietly as not to alert the young lady of his thoughts. Surprisingly enough, the woman seemed very intelligent, and she was certainly knowledgeable of the store. BC Chay's had a wide selection of clothes to fit a young person's mood with a ghetto twist or not being to ghetto. She put together an outfit for D.J. that accented his bronze skin and manly features. D.J. walked out of the store, not only with a dope outfit to wear to the concert but also genuinely learning the meaning of the old cliché, 'you can't judge a book by its cover.'

D.J. was nervous as he pulled up to the concert hall. He didn't know what to expect. He only sang to Zodana and the rest of the audience that night at the club, but he hadn't really had a conversation with her. He was hoping this night would go right. Trip teased him, on the way out of the house, telling him that he could sing, but him dealing with a woman, he was not "all that." Even though D.J. hated to admit it, he knew it was true. Even in the cold night air, D.J.'s hands still grew sweaty.

As he entered the door, he had a notion of turning around. He still couldn't believe that Zodana wanted to see him. He knew that he would hate himself forever if he passed up an opportunity like this. He felt very anxious to find out why she had left him the note. He was met by security. It seemed that security was really tight. He gave the security guard his name, and it appeared that his name was on the list because he was motioned to follow the guard down a narrow, but well-lit hall. They gave him a clearance badge to slip around his neck. D.J. was nervous, but it was too late now; the guard was knocking on the door. When the guard heard "come in," he pushed the door open and informally announced D.J. He walked into the bright smile of Zodana, and what a smile it was! She had her dreaded soft curls pulled back as she was having make-up added to her face by her personal make-up artist.

"Hello, Dexton, how are you?"

"How did you know my name was Dexton, oh excuse my rudeness, hello, Zodana." D.J. couldn't believe it, he was actually blushing.

"A woman knows how to find out things when she is interested."

"Interested in what?" D.J. said shyly.

"You!" Zodana smiled at D.J.

D.J. was a handsome brother but really didn't realize it. He never noticed that most women thought that he was cute. He didn't know where the conversation was going, and so he abruptly changed it.

"So, are you nervous?" D.J. asked.

"Yeah, I always get nervous, but there is no better feeling in the world than on stage, giving an audience part of the spirit that you have inside."

"I know what you mean, but I've never experienced the type of crowd that you have and about to sing for."

"Don't worry, with a voice like yours, it won't be too long."

"Thank you, I appreciate that."

"I mean it, you have a great voice, and I enjoyed listening to you the other night."

"Come on now, you are going to make me get beside myself." D.J. smiled. Zodana's comments seemed to make him light up.

"I guess you are wondering why I left you the note." I was genuinely impressed with your voice, and I was telling my manager and producer about you."

"What? You don't even know me, and you would do that for me? You seem to have a lot of faith in someone that you don't know."

"Look, someone helped me by allowing me to share my gift with the world, and I think that I have to help someone else."

"So, what exactly are you saying to me?" D.J. said, almost about to float off the ground.

"What I'm saying is that I want them to talk with you."

"Oh, my God!" D.J. put his hand over his mouth after a quick shout. "Thank you, thank you, and thank you!"

Zodana smiled at D.J.'s happiness and remembered that she had the same expression when she got the news at the start of her career.

"Okay, I have arranged a seat for you out front. Go out there, and I will talk to you after the concert."

"Cool, I'll see you afterward," D.J. said.

The concert had already started, and Jai-Waye was "tearing it down." D.J. found his seat and enjoyed the show. The artist's combination on stage and the thoughts of his own appearance on stage made him plaster a cheesy smile on his face. Zodana finally took the stage after a remarkable performance from Tommy Phillipe'.

Her voice wowed the crowd. After the second upbeat song, Zodana decided to slow it down. Then she spoke the words that D.J. would remember for a lifetime.

"I would like to take the time to introduce you to a rising star. I had a chance to hear this gentleman sing, and he is one to watch." Zodana was truly giving D.J. some strong props.

"His name is Mr. Dexton Cumming, better known as D.J. Come on up here, man, and let my people see you." D.J., in sheer disbelief, hopped up on the stage and stood beside Zodana. He took a bow as if he had done something. Zodana motioned for the stagehands to bring a stool for D.J. to sit on. D.J. sat on the seat as she started her song.

Let me love you tonight and get that body right.
It's a long time coming, and I can't wait to be with you.

Zodana put D.J. in a trance with her words that seem to shoot straight through his heart. Then she did something that D.J. was not expecting,

"Sing a little bit of this for me, D.J. I know that you know the words." D.J. was awestruck, but he took the mic and began to sing. The crowd went wild as he began to sing. He knew that he was truly home on the stage. This is where he belonged, where he truly felt free. When he gave the mic back to Zodana, she asked the audience to provide him with a round of applause, but they had never stopped clapping. D.J. would always remember this night, or what was in the store to come for him. He was about to blow up.

Kendall and Jason made it back to the apartment soaking wet. When it rained in the city of New York, it really rained. The fellows made it back drenched from the downpour. It started raining in the middle of their one-on-one basketball game. They would have stopped when the rain started, but there was a bet of one hundred dollars involved. Jason waited as Kendall went to get a towel from the hall closet for him. Kendall didn't want him to track a trail of rainwater throughout the house.

"Here, dude, take off those wet clothes and leave them at the door. I think that I have some extra clothes that you can put on after you have dried off." Kendall said.

"Cool, but don't bring me no hand-me-down stuff that you don't even like to wear."

"Man, I don't have any clothes like that. All of my clothes are fly." Kendall said with a cocky attitude. Kendall went to the room and pulled off all of his clothes, dried himself off, and then headed to the dresser to find some clothes for himself and Jason. He must have taken a good minute because Jason walked back into the room, nude. When Kendall turned around, he dropped the clothes on the floor from shock.

"Did I scare you, man?" Jason said.

"Naw, man, you just caught me off guard." Kendall felt slightly breathless "I just don't like niggas sneaking up on me."

"Nigga, who you calling a nigga?" "You, punk!" Kendall said jokingly.

Kendall picked up the clothes and threw them at Jason. Jason quickly dressed in Kendall's old half-cut football shirt and practice shorts from his football days at Grambling and went into the living room and turned on the television.

"Hey, I'm gonna take a quick shower, and I'll be right out," Kendall said.

"Alright, I'll be looking for a game on the T.V.

Kendall walked into the bathroom and closed the door behind him. He sat on the edge of the tub in total confusion. In that slight moment of Jason's nudeness, Kendall felt a tingling feeling inside himself. He knew that this was not happening. His penis started to arouse as Kendall thought about Jason's healthy masculine body standing before him. He never had an inkling that he was attracted to men all of his life, but it seemed that he felt something for Jason. "Man, what the hell is going on with me? Kendall had to admit that in the past two weeks, he had really gotten close to Jason. He really helped him through some tough times. Kendall went back to work, continued looking for new acting gigs, and started to get his life back on track. He found himself getting closer to Jason than he had to any of the members of the pack. Maybe Jason was his best friend. Perhaps the attraction was just the comfort and help that Jason provided for him. He damn sure couldn't tell the pack the problems he had been through, and Jason was the one person that Kendall could talk with about his top secrets.

Kendall finished showering and went back into the living room to watch television. The clock on the wall said 8:45 p.m. He looked out the window to find that it was still pouring down rain. Jason was lying on his back, fully asleep. Kendall stared at him for about five long minutes. He had to admit to himself that he found Jason attractive. His rough face with its high cheekbones, hard rock chest, and bulging biceps, and the print of his manhood against the material of his shorts. Kendall sighed, got a blanket from the closet, and placed it over his boy. Then he went back into the bedroom to watch television so he would not disturb Jason. Kendall started to get out one of those cigarettes he used when his mind was perplexed, but he decided against it. He turned on the television, got under the covers, and could not refrain from thinking about Jason. Kendall couldn't find anything on T.V., so he turned it off and turned on the radio connected to the alarm clock beside the bed. He heard the voice of Ped' east coming across the radio and knew that it was the quiet hour and nothing but love songs would be coming through the radio. Kendall smiled to himself and tried to go to sleep, although he knew that it would be impossible. It was now about 10:40 p.m., and Kendall still could not sleep. He was running with his thoughts when he heard the stir in the living room. He listened to the quiet steps as they came down the hallway. Jason went into the room and called Kendall.

"Hey, Kendall, Yo, Kendall. I am about to leave, man."

"Hey, man, you can stay if you like. It is still raining pretty hard, and you do stay on the other side of town."

"Yeah, I know, but I don't want to put you out."

"It is the least that I can do for all of the help and support that you have given me in the past three weeks."

Jason walked into the room and sat on the bed beside Kendall. The light from the billboard shone through the room, giving the friends enough light to catch a faint glimpse of each other.

"No sweat, man, I have had the time of my life hanging with you, dude."

"I do have to admit that I thought you were going to walk right out of the door when you learned about my little escapade."

"Man, I would never do that to a friend."

"I am glad. I just don't know what I would have done without you."

"Thanks, my nigga."

"Nigga, I thought that you didn't like that word?"

"No, I said that I don't like being called one."

"What? And so you are going to call me one."

Kendall jumped up and thumped Jason on the back of the head. Jason, in his surprise, grabbed Kendall playfully and started to wrestle with him. Kendall was not a small man, but Jason was slightly larger. Within seconds, Jason had Kendall pinned down on the bed.

"Do you give up, man?" Jason said, "I can't hear you, speak louder!"

Kendall felt Jason's hardening penis against his stomach as he was straddling him to hold him down. Kendall could not believe what was going on. Across the radio came the sounds of Anita Baker's *You Bring Me Joy*. Kendall felt his own penis starting to rise, and he knew that Jason could feel it. Jason stopped the roughness, but could not figure out what was going on or what was about to happen. Neither did Kendall. Jason leaned down and kissed Kendall on the side of his neck, his cheek, and then his lips. Kendall's heart started to pace faster and faster. The mixture of Jason's smell and the sweet sounds of Ms. Baker totally aroused him. He found that he was actually kissing Jason back.

Jason never gave him an idea he was interested in him, but Kendall knew that he had the thought all along or at least for a while. Kendall couldn't lie to himself. He found an instant enjoyment of the moment. He really wanted to stop himself because, in his mind, he knew it was wrong, but his body and heart were saying something different. Jason placed his hand across Kendall's brow and slid it down the side of his face. Jason continued to run his hand down Kendall's neck and stopped around his chest to caress his hardened nipples. Kendall thought that he would explode instantly. From the light of the billboard, Jason's silhouette seemed to set Kendall afire. Jason leaned once again and kissed Kendall's nipples.

Without hesitation or resistance, the guys began to give themselves to each other in a frenzy of passion. To Kendall, it didn't feel the same as it had the night that he betrayed himself at Deacon's studio. Jason's touch was a warm welcome to his yearning sexuality. It just felt so right. Jason didn't seem to have any reservations about being with Kendall, and Kendall released himself to the pleasures of Jason's touch. Jason began to remove Kendall's boxers, and to his surprise, there was no resistance. Again, Jason kissed along the side of his neck, then his broad shoulders, in-between his chest until he found his happy trail of hair that led him to the grand prize. Kendall moaned with excitement and grabbed Jason by the top of his head, giving him the okay to feel free to explore. This feeling was new and magical, Kendall squeezed his eyes tight to make sure that no moments escaped him. He wanted to remember it all as Jason released his body to sexual ecstasy.

These two large masculine guys fulfilled each other in peaceful silence. Neither of them knew where this lovemaking would end, but they couldn't stop the feeling that ran through their bodies.

Jason continued to explore Kendall's body. The smooth curves of his manhood excited Jason. His chiseled chest was inviting, and Jason licked every part of it. Kendall held his head back in awe of the feelings that were taking over his body. As Jason lowered his luscious lips to Kendall's hard penis. He found himself, a man, enjoying sensations given to him by another man. Jason's warm mouth on his shaft was phenomenal. Nothing in his past, as he remembered it, brought him so much pleasure. He knew that he had to return the favor.

Kendall flipped Jason over roughly and grabbed him by the throat and kissed him passionately. He licked Jason from his chin and stopped briefly to caress his muscular pecs, and then he did it, and Jason entered his mouth. "Oh my god! Am I really doing this? Is there a penis in my mouth?" Kendall thought. It was so surreal, but this moment was too intense to let his mind overshadow what his body craved. Kendall had been sexually active for years, but this was so different, but it felt so good, so right. In his mind, he didn't know how far he would go, but he was willing to try with Jason. In sweat and pleasure, they covered each other in a new experience.

After the experience was over, the men lay in silence on the warm sheets for a long time. Their naked bodies perfectly accented against the soft white sheets with their faces in different directions was like a painting at an art gallery. Neither of them knew what to say or even if there was anything to say. Kendall knew that all of his feelings about what he did was the same, but it felt so different from Jason. Maybe it was because he treasured his friendship. Perhaps it was because Kendall needed someone to hold him and make him feel better, someone who cared about his needs and wants. Maybe he was vulnerable after the whole ordeal at Deac's place. Kendall didn't know what the answer was; all he knew was that he felt something special with Jason and could not explain it. He wasn't even sure what Jason was thinking, but it was killing him, so he had to ask.

"Jason, man, what are you thinking?" Kendall said. There was a pause for what seemed a minute, and then Jason spoke.

"I don't really know what I am thinking. I guess I feel like I am making life more complicated for you and now for myself."

"What is that supposed to mean?"

"What I mean is, and maybe I shouldn't say this, but I like you a lot like my friend and my brother, but I can't ignore that there are some other feelings that I have for you and I can't quite put my finger on what it is."

Kendall was speechless. Maybe Jason had been thinking about this for a while.

"Man, I am confused," Kendall said, turning around in the bed.

"But what we just did didn't make me feel guilty, it makes me understand that I can allow myself to be open. Certainly, I am not a faggot, and I hope that name is never attached to me, but I feel something for you."

The guys started to chuckle lightly as Kendall reached over and kissed Jason softly on the lips.

"I don't think that we have to explain ourselves. I have never been into having a relationship with a guy, so I think that we should take this thing one day at a time." Jason said.

"I feel you. I really don't think that we should ever tell anyone about this." Kendall said.

"Are you crazy? Why would we? You know that people would never understand." Jason's voice seemed concerned about the notion.

"I heard that. We are consenting adults, and we don't owe anyone anything. Let's just take it slow." Kendall said.

"Cool, are we on again for some hoops tomorrow? I want to win back my money," Jason said with the biggest grin ever.

"Yeah, man, it's on!"

After having made one of the most significant decisions of their lives, the two men fell asleep in each other's arms.

Ped' east rang the doorbell to Jessica's house. He had done his research and found out where she lived, just like she had done some weeks before. He was as nervous as a virgin on prom night. Ped' east had walked away from the door five times before he decided to ring the bell. He didn't know if another man was living with her, but after the money he spent going home and the hotel, he had to see where this would lead. Even though he was at home in Baton Rouge, he didn't let any of his relatives know. He was there on a mission, and he didn't need all the questions to follow if his people knew he was in town.

Ped' east could hear someone approaching the door. When the door opened, it was Jessica. She was just so breath-taking every time that he saw her. His knees began to grow weak, and he thought that he was going to fall. Her facial expressions let him know that she was just as surprised as he was when he came home and found her in his apartment.

"Peddy, what are you doing here?" Jessica said, revealing the surprise in her voice.

"I just had to see you. I couldn't believe that you left the way that you did. There are so many things that we enjoyed and talked about. How could you just leave me again?" "I thought that you respected me more than that?" Ped' east couldn't understand the emotion in his voice, but his cup was full, and it had started to run over.

"I didn't mean to hurt you, but it was time for me to leave."

"Well, can I come in and talk with you, or should I just leave?"

"Excuse my manners, of course, you can come in."

"Thank you." Ped' east smiled slightly.

He was very anxious to see where this journey would take him. He followed Jessica into her beautiful home. Jessica always had good taste. Even in college, she didn't have a lot of money, but she was still the one to make something out of nothing, and the place was no less than perfect. This time, he could tell that Jessica had some money. Ped' east was happy to know that she was doing well for herself. She led him into a small cozy family room where they could talk. The room was decorated quite nicely. Ped' east was impressed. She offered him something to drink, but he refused. He just wanted to talk, to get some answers for her appearance after so many years and then her disappearance suddenly as she had come.

"Peddy, I can't believe that you came here."

"I can't believe that you left like you did."

"Okay, I am sorry for that, but something came up, and I had to leave. I really didn't know how to do it, but I needed to leave."

"Why couldn't you just have said that?" "It is not as simple as it seems, Peddy." Ped' east started to feel himself getting a little upset at Jessica's responses.

"I don't see the complexity in it. Common courtesy is something that anybody deserves."

"I wasn't trying to hurt you or anything. I just didn't know how to handle it."

"Come on, Jessica. You come waltzing into my life after all of these years" Ped' east could feel his temperature rising, "and you hadn't planned out what you were doing? That sounds a little crazy to me. Why didn't you just wait longer to get yourself together before you just came stepping back into my life?" Ped' east didn't even know that he was now standing, and his voice was getting louder by every word. "You just can't keep doing this to me. I have feelings too!"

"Mommy, who is this, and why is he yelling at you?" This soft voice came from the child standing in the doorway. The child seemed startled at the stranger who was in his house. The water seemed to form in his little eyes from not recognizing the man and hearing his mother's disrespect.

"It's okay, Peddy, baby, go back to bed." Instantly Jessica's voice was soft and motherly. She walked toward the little boy to console him. He hugged her leg, never taking his eyes off Ped' east. Ped' east was shocked to hear Jessica's words.

On the other hand, Jessica seemed to also be speechless, but words did come from her lips. "Ped' east, I would like for you to say hello to P.J., your son." Jessica waited in silence to see what reaction Ped' east was going to have.

Ped' east seemed stunned by what he had seen and heard. "What? What are you talking about?" Ped' east, as well, had never taken his eyes off the child. "I don't understand." He felt as if he was dreaming.

"Well, I really don't know where to start. There is so much that I need to tell you, but I really don't know where to start."

"How about from the beginning."

"Okay, let me put P.J. back in bed first."

"No, please! Let him stay for a little while."

"I didn't know what to do when I got pregnant. I felt like my world was closing in around me. I know that I should have said something, but I couldn't. I felt like I had let my parents down and myself. I didn't know what to do with a baby, and I knew that you didn't need the hassle. I was the one that my entire family depended on to make something out of myself. I was the one that my parents measured my brothers and sisters against. I was so lost Ped' east; I didn't know what to do.

I didn't have any answers in my head other than to run, so one night, it just got too hard to deal with, and I left. I just jumped on a bus that was headed in whatever direction it would take me."

"I don't understand, Jessica. You never gave me the option to be there for you. You never gave me a choice as to whether I wanted to be responsible or not. If you loved me so much, how could you just walk out of my life and stay away all of these years?"

"I don't know, Peddy. I was young, stupid, and confused. I think about that night every day of my life. I didn't know what to do, and I was not in the state of mind that I could really think it through." Jessica was crying now, and the tears softened Ped' east.

"Why did you decide to come to me after all of these years?"

"I made my peace with everyone except you. It was hard, but my parents and I have started a new relationship. They love P.J., and I just knew that you had to know. All I know is that I love this little boy to death, and he deserved to have a chance at a relationship with his father. I didn't know exactly how I would do that but was going to give it my best shot. I enjoyed the time that we had when I was in New York, but I knew that it would come to an end."

"But why did it have to come to an end, Jessica?"

"My mom called. P.J. got sick, and I knew the vacation was over. After all that time we spent together, I thought that it could be right, I could be right, I could make it right." Jessica was crying harder now. Little Peddy started to hold tight to his mother.

"Mommy, don't cry!" Ped' east was touched by the emotion that he saw in the child. Ped' east was stopped in his tracks when he really looked into the eyes of the child. The little boy looked just like him. He knew that the right thing to do was to have a blood test, but there was no way to deny that this child was his.

"Come on, Jessica, don't cry. I don't mean to upset you. I came all of this way because I love you, and I can't think of any other person who I would rather be with."

Jessica started to smile through the tears. In all of these years, she dreamt about this day but never thought that it would happen.

"Hey, Lil' Peddy, come here." The little boy seemed frightened.

"It's okay, baby, you don't have to be afraid; this is your daddy. His name is Ped' east. Jessica comforted the little boy.

"Hey, mommy, he has the same name that I do."

"Yes, he does sweetheart, this is your father," Jessica said again. They both smiled at each other.

"Come here, son," Ped' east reached for the little boy. Slowly the little boy detached himself from his mother and started his way toward Ped' east. Ped' east was able to get a hold of the little boy, and he held him in his arms. The little boy smelled so good. Ped' east didn't know if any fatherly instincts would kick in even if he had them, but holding this child really felt good.

"Nice to meet you, daddy," P.J. said. Ped' east thought that his heart would burst.

Jessica's tears were flowing, and she had no reason to stop them. This was one of the happiest days of her life. Ped' east knew that they had a lot of talk about, but he was sure that everything would work out.

CHAPTER TEN

· · · · · · · · ●· · · · · · · ·

This winter was one of the coldest that the guys experienced in New York. They loved calling New York home, but this freezing weather was one thing that they could not get used to. D.J. and Trip were on their way to the legendary "Apollo" theatre. They were really excited. They watched the show on television for years, and now they were about to experience it firsthand. They both had their reasons for wanting to be on the show. Trip wanted the feeling of dancing on the stage of the Apollo. D.J. imagined a thousand times how he would walk from behind the curtain, rub the log of good luck, and then sing the audience into another world. The whisk, the cold wind, brought both of the guys back to reality.

"D.J., I never told you about the time that I was on the subway, and I was almost scared shitless, did I?"

"No, but I am sure that you are going to tell me."

"Come on fool, don't act like I talk you to death, and you don't want to hear what a brotha got to say."

"I am not saying that at all; go ahead and tell your story, man!"

"Well, I was on the subway on Sunday. I was trying to get to Greenwich Village to meet this little "hottie" at the club when I heard this cup and the rattling change. I had learned that it is less hassle to give the bums some money, and they won't harass you. Anyway, I was waiting to give the bum some coins because I heard the noise getting closer. I turned around when I heard the sound of the coins right on me. I didn't see anyone, but I continued to listen to the coins clanging together. Man, I looked down, and suddenly, I saw a man with no legs up to his hip on a skateboard pushing with one hand while shaking the cup with the other. That shit freaked me out, and

I instantly jumped, dropping the change all over the subway around me. People started laughing at me. I guess that they were used to the bum, but I sure as hell wasn't. I got off at the first stop we made. I was miles from where I needed to be, but I just waited for another train to come, and I took that one because I was so embarrassed and shook up.

Trip heard D.J. laughing at him, and it started to make him angry. "I know that you are not laughing at me, nigga?" Trip said with a sly smile.

"You damn straight, I am."

"That's ain't funny, dude."

"You are a lie. That is hella funny!"

Trip picked up some of the snow from the ground and threw it at D.J. "Oh, no, you didn't, you Lil' nigga!" D.J. threw back at him. It was on then. It was strange to see two grown men throwing snow at each other, but it was entertaining for the brothers. It was the kind of relief they needed.

The fellas finally made it to the theater. They were both just as excited as two kids in a candy store. This was a moment in history for them. To be in the Apollo theatre was a dream come true. The brothers walked into the theatre and started to look around.

"Damn, this shit is a lot smaller than I thought that it would be." Trip said with a puzzled look on his face.

"Yeah, it is a little small, huh?"

"I cannot believe that this little rickety ass place is the famous Apollo Theatre. Damn!"

"Come on, Trip, it's not that bad. Have some respect."

"I know that you have got to be kidding me. All my life, I dreamed of coming to the Apolllllloooooooo Theater, and this is the shit I see."

"Think about it this way. There were so many stars who were born right here. The culture of an entire people was birthed within the walls of this theatre. Dreams became a reality here." D.J. sounded almost poetic.

"Damn, you ought to do a commercial for them." Trip said sarcastically.

"You always have something negative to say."

"Look, don't get mad at me because this place is a matchbox!"

I didn't do it. Trip knew that he was starting to get on D.J.'s nerves with all of his comments, but he loved doing that to him.

He was so sensitive.

"Come on, Trip, don't miss the forest for the trees."

"Hell, you couldn't get a forest in here."

Both men started to laugh as they walked to their seats just as the show was about to begin. Thirty minutes into the show, both of the brothers realized that they loved the atmosphere of the place. It was vibrant with heritage. The guys imagined themselves on stage, and the crowds were going wild. Even during the icy cold weather, it was a good night for the brothers to hang out.

Part Four:

I'm my own man

Chapter Eleven

· · · · · · ● · · · · · · ·

Click, click, snap, snap. Trip was turned and positioned at every angle the camera could focus on. He had successfully gotten the position as the premier model for the *SemajE* hip-hop clothes line industry. He was modeling everything from leisurewear to underwear. Trip was not the biggest model in the industry, but he was on his way. He was still dancing with Joya Reynolds, but when the modeling job came about, it seemed more stable, so he decided to put the dancing on hold for a minute until he could really get his feet planted.

Trip had finally moved out of his brother's apartment and now had a place of his own. Even though his brother wanted him to stay, Trip wanted to prove to him, the pack, his deceased parents, and especially to himself that he was a man that could take care of himself.

The photo shoot was over, and from the look on the photographer's face, she was pleased. Trip walked off the set and was met by one of the other models under the company.

"Yo, Trip, are you still going to the party with me?" Jeremy said.

"Man, I don't really feel like going."

"Come on, man, don't punk out on me. All the hunnies are going to be at this party, and you know that they will be waiting to look into your grown face.

"Okay, but only because I think that it will help my career."

"Well, it damn sure could not hurt it. You are the poster boy for *SemajE*, and you know that. Now stop tripping."

Trip was at the party, but he really was not enjoying himself. He didn't know why, but he really had an urge to just go home. He had a couple of drinks to relax his mind, but that didn't seem to help. He was still really not feeling it. Jeremy walked over to him.

"Come on, man, I see you over here by yourself, and all of the finest women are asking about you. Come on, I want to show you something." Jeremy said.

Trip walked with Jeremy's arm around his shoulder like he was a little child comforted by his father. Jeremy led Trip to the back part of the building. It seemed to be very secluded.

"Now what I am about to show you will either really impress you or blow your mind, hell it might do both."

"Man, what are you talking about? I am not a child, and you don't have to treat me like that."

"Come on, man, don't be so sensitive." Jeremy opened the small door that faced him. Trip's eyes flew open. He was definitely awake now. Inside of the room was huge ballers, naked women, and plenty of nose candy. As they walked into the room. A woman walked past Trip and grabbed his behind. Trip jumped from the tug of his derrière. He had never seen anything like this in his life.

"Come on, man, let's get this party started," Jeremy whispered to Trip.

Jeremy walked Trip over to a table that was full of cocaine. Jeremy used his pinky fingernail to scoop up some of the drugs and inhaled it into his nose. Trip could not believe what he had just done.

"Come on, man, dig in."

"Man, I have never done drugs, are you crazy?"

"Then try just a little. It will get you loose so that you can start to have a little fun."

"I don't know about this, Jeremy. I…"

"Come on, man, stop acting like a little bitch! I wouldn't play you. I am just trying to set you off. Do you think that everyone gets to come back into this area? Some people have been to several of these parties and know nothing about this room. This is your first one, and I bring you back here. Some important people could help your career blow up." Jeremy threw the ball into Trip's court, hoping that he would return the serve.

Trip looked strangely around the room and thought to himself, *"What the hell! One time never hurt anyone."* He leaned down and sniffed some of the nose candy without ever answering Jeremy.

Trip coughed heavily while grabbing his nose. Jeremy and a few of the other people laughed at him. Trip fell back onto the couch directly behind him. He seemed to instantly be in space.

"Give it a second. You will feel good in a hot second."

Trip started to giggle. He really didn't know why, but everything seemed to be funny to him. Jeremy walked over to two of the ladies that were nearby. He whispered into their ears, but Trip could not figure out what they were saying. Trip could see the ladies walking toward him through the crowd of people dancing in the open space, but he seemed to have slightly lost control of himself. His vision was blurred. The ladies slid next to him on the couch. One of them appeared to whisper in his ear, but instead, she lightly nibbled on his ear. Trip laid his head back and let the woman continue to nibble. Trip didn't notice until it was too late that the other woman had unbuckled his pants and had exposed his penis. Before he knew it, the woman started to send Trip to places the drugs couldn't. In Trip's mind, he tried to rationalize what was happening and why, in the presence of the people. But, between the warm lips and teeth on his ear and the warm moisture that surrounded his penis, Trip couldn't logically piece together what was going on, and so he let the inevitable happen. The ladies pulled him off the couch and into the bathroom nearby. The last thing that Jeremy saw before seeing the door close was Trip's pants and underwear around his ankles, and as one of the women was mounting him, the other straddled his face. Jeremy laughed at his friend and walked back over to the table of nose candy.

"Happy Birthday to you! Happy Birthday to you, Happy Birthday dear, P.J., Happy Birthday to you... Yeaaaaaa!"

This was the first Birthday that Ped' east had spent with his son in the five years of his life. He didn't exactly know what he was feeling, but it really felt good. There were fifteen children there with all of their mothers. There was one father that was there probably wishing he could be someplace else other than in a room full of women watching a little boy blow the candles out on a cake. Jessica's parents were also there. They were sending mixed signals. Ped' east wasn't sure if they were excited about him being in their daughter's life, especially now being there for P.J., or they just thought that he would be like all of the other fathers in the world and leave again. Ped' east knew that he would be there for his son. When the test came back, and it showed that he was 99.9%, the father of P.J., he was overjoyed. It really didn't matter though, the first time that he laid eyes on that little boy, he knew that P.J. was his son.

"I did it, daddy, I did it! I blew out all the candles on my cake!" P.J. said to Ped' east. Ped' east though that his heart would explode with emotion. His son had taken to him so quickly, and he loved every moment of it.

"You sure did, little man." Ped' east picked him up and swung him around. All of the ladies at the party started with the *Awwwww*, and they crowded around Jessica talking in secret, saying, "That was the sweetest thing that they had ever seen."

"Okay, man…Let's cut this cake so that you and your little homies can have some."

"I'll get that," Jessica said.

"Kay, thanks," Ped' east said with a smile.

"What are you smiling about?"

"Nothing." Ped' east really was happy. Jessica was a beautiful woman, and she had allowed him to have a son. Even though it didn't start out good, it seemed as if everything was going to be alright.

"Hey, Jessica, I'll be right back. I have a phone call to make in the next room."

"Is everything all right?"

"Yeah, where is your dad?"

"He is out at the back on the bar-b-que grill."

"Cool." Ped' east walked off with a sly smile. Ped' east found Mr. Harvey out in the back. He took a deep breath and walked toward him. The smoke coming from the grill was delightful. Ped' east had not smelled the aroma of down south food in a long time, and he really missed it. There were a few places in New York that claimed to serve southern food, but if you are from the south, you know that it is nothing like what you are accustomed to.

"Hey, Mr. Harvey, can I talk with you for a moment?"

"Yeah, son, go ahead."

Well, I know that you know about everything that has happened to this point. I don't want you to think that I won't take care of P.J. I didn't know that I had a son and I know that doesn't change the fact that I have not been in his life, but I promise you that I will give him the best of everything that I can."

"Son, I don't blame you. From what I understand, you didn't know, but I do want to say that because you all wanted to play grown when you were not, it caused us to lose Jessica for a while."

"I realize that, sir, and I apologize to you for that."

"Well, you know, in my old age, I have learned a few things. I have learned that life is a mofo, and if you don't learn how to deal with it and all of the blows that it sends your way, you end up TKO in the first round. And, even if you recover, you end up Muhammad Ali, living the rest of your life only a shell of the man you used to be."

Ped' east didn't know if he understood the analogy that Mr. Harvey was giving him, but he had always learned to let your elders talk, even if it was a lengthy conversation, and it wasn't about much.

"Thank you for understanding. I want to ask you something, though."

"Okay, shoot."

"Do you mind if I ask your daughter to marry me?" Mr. Harvey tried to pretend like he was not excited, but he was, and Ped' east could tell.

"Look, I don't want you to think that Jessica or P.J. is not well taken care of. That daughter of mine is a strong woman. I raised her to be that way. If you are just doing this because you are in a moment, then I don't want you to mess up their lives."

"No! It's nothing like that. I really love your daughter and I always have. Even when I was in denial with her leaving me and coming back, I knew that I loved her. She is my soulmate, and I know that. But, being the upstanding man that you are, I knew that I had to get your permission first."

"Well......okay, you have my blessing, but just know that if you ever hurt my little girl," Mr. Harvey said with a slight smile, "You see this hot dog on the grill...this is the same place yours will be, and I will feed it to you when it's done." Ped' east thought that was a terrible visual, but he knew that he had won over Mr. Harvey. Ped' east reached in his pocket and pulled out the ring that he had gone out and bought. He showed it to his future father-in-law the three-carat, square cut, a pink diamond with small diamonds in the band. He had a lump in his throat, waiting for Mr. Harvey to respond.

"Hey, you got good taste, boy. When are you going to propose?"

Ped' east let out a sigh of relief. "Right now, I just wanted you to approve."

"Damn, hold up and let me take these last few hot dogs off the grill." Mr. Harvey seemed excited, and that made Ped' east at ease.

Ped' east knew that everything would be alright as long as Jessica said yes. He had just won over Mr. Harvey, and he knew it. He really felt like his life was coming together. The children were coated with cake and ice-cream. All of the mothers were on their jobs of wiping down children and trying to brush off the embarrassment that their child had given them. Ped' east took another deep breath and walked toward Jessica and P.J.

"Hey Jessica, I have to talk with you about something."

"Yeah?"

"Hey, everyone, listen up. I have an announcement to make, and I want all of you to hear it." Ped' east felt a lump in his throat, but he knew that he could do this, and he really wanted to. Mr. Harvey had entered the house, and he was standing beside Mrs. Harvey.

"What is it Ped' east, what is wrong?"

"Nothing is wrong, sweetheart, nothing at all is wrong."

"Well, what is going on?" Jessica started to get really inquisitive.

"Shhhhhh, just listen." Ped' east took a deep breath.

"Jessica, these past two months have been the best in my life. I was able to find you, I was able to look into the face of my beautiful son, and I don't think that I ever want to miss out on any more birthdays." Ped' east lowered himself to one knee. He wanted to make sure that he did everything right. Ped' east knew that the pack was going to trip because he didn't tell them that he was going to do all of this, but he never felt so sure.

"Hey, P.J., come here." Ped' east wanted his son by his side. P.J. came and sat on his daddy's lap.

"Jessica, will you marry me?" There was dead silence in the room. All of the girlfriends in the room were feeling two different emotions. They were either fairy tale happy or jealous as hell! Either way, Jessica was in total shock by the gesture.

"Are you for real?"

"Yes, baby, I am for real." Ped' east pulled out the ring and handed it to her.

"Oh My God! Yes, Peddy, I will, I will." Ped' east jumped up with P.J. in his arms and gave Jessica a big hug. There were tears of joy everywhere. The ladies even started clapping. Mr. Harvey was clapping as well.

"I love you, Peddy!"

"I love you too, sweet baby!" The parents seemed really proud as they were hugging each other in tears. Everything was coming back into the order that it should have been in the first place.

CHAPTER TWELVE

• • • • • • •• ● • • • • • • •

D.J. sat on the balcony of his apartment in just his terrycloth bathroom. The cool breeze on his hairy chest after a hot shower always seemed to be the therapy he needed before going to the club. D.J. poured himself a glass of Merlot to the sounds of Miles Davis, thinking about the offer that was on the table for him. Zodana hooked him up, and he was waiting to sign on her label. He had been to the studio several times and had some of his demos being played frequently throughout the city. He was even being booked at other clubs and opened once for Zodana. The two had actually become great friends. *"A toast to you, D.J. You have worked really hard, and it seems that everything was starting to pay off. You are on your way, man!"* D.J. lifted his glass as if he were toasting with someone else. *"Mom and Dad, I hope that you are proud. Trip and I are taking care of business. I love you both, and I will never forget all of the things that you taught me. I will also never let Trip forget them either."* D.J. felt a tear form in his eye as he remembered the love and nurturing of his parents. He drank the wine and laid his head back to enjoy the trickle of the wine down his throat and the tears that slid his cheeks.

There was a knock at the door. D.J. really hated to be disturbed during this moment, but he would answer it anyway. He wiped his face, tightened his bathroom, and walked toward the door. When D.J. got to the door and opened it, he found that no one was there. At the bottom of the door was a bouquet of flowers; he smiled at the notion of being sent flowers. He picked up the flowers, carried them into the house, and placed them on the table. He pulled the card that was attached to the flowers and read the note inside. *A Secret Admirer.* D.J. smiled as he thought to himself who it could be that sent the flowers. He had only had one person that he even had some communications with. She was indeed a friend to him. She had helped him to make his dreams more than just a closed eye fantasy. They were actively becoming a reality. He appreciated the gesture and wanted to give her a call to thank her for the gesture.

As he was reaching for the phone, it rang.

"Hello?"

"Hey D.J., this is Ped' east."

"Yo, what's up, dude?"

"I did it."

"You did what, nigga?"

"I asked Jessica to marry me, and she said Yes!"

"What? Good going, man. When is the big date?"

"I don't know, but really soon. We are not going to have that big wedding. Just a few of our best friends and family."

"Ahh…you little shit. I didn't think that you were that serious. I am proud of you, man."

"Hey man, I feel good, and I have you to thank for it. You talked me into going after Jessica."

"I'm really happy for you, man."

"Ahh, guess what?"

"What, man?"

"I have a son!"

"Well shut the front door, are you serious?"

"Yep, that was the reason that she left back in college, she was pregnant and embarrassed."

"You seem really excited, man!"

"I am, he looks just like me, eyes and all! And, his name is P.J., Ped' east Jr."

"Dang, son, you left one and came back three, huh?"

"I guess you can say that."

"Well, as long as you are happy, I'm happy."

"Thanks, man, I will talk with you real soon."

"Okay, man, later."

"Hey, D.J.!"

"Yeah"

"I love you, brother. Thank you for always being there for me."

"I love you too, man, be blessed."

"Later."

Kendall sat on the floor, glistening in sweat. He had just finished his workout. His favorite T.V. show came on a back-to-back, and that always gave him an hour to get in a good workout before going to bed. But, tonight, he was not going to bed, he was going out. Kendall was finally getting his life back together, thanks to Jason. He booked two commercials that were airing regularly and a small part in a Broadway production. His relationship with Jason was helping him to give his life some structure. He felt more motivated, and Jason was the boost to his confidence that he needed. Kendall really felt good about himself.

Tonight, he and Jason were going to see D.J. at the club. It seemed that it had been ages since he had been to see his boy sing. D.J. had called him and asked him to come. D.J. would be leaving passes for them at the front door. He said that he had someone extraordinary that he wanted him to meet. There was some vital information that he wanted to tell everyone, and so he wanted the whole pack to be there. The phone rang. Kendall got up to answer it.

"Hello."

"What is up, Ken, it's Ped' east."

"I know your voice when I hear it, clown."

"What's up, man? Are you coming to the club tonight?"

"Yeah, I will be there."

"Hey, do you need me to pick you up?"

"Naw, I am going to catch a ride with Jason."

"Jason?"

"Yeah, why? You don't want him to come?"

"When did y'all get so tight?"

"What do you mean?"

"I mean, every time that I talk with you, you are either with Jason or about to be with Jason. You haven't found yourself a new best friend, have you?"

"Naw, fool!"

"Okay, I don't wanna have to call a pack meeting." Ped' east was joking with Kendall.

"You are so stupid. I'll see you at the club."

"Cool, dude, see you in a minute."

Kendall hung up the phone and went to the refrigerator to get some cold water to quench his vast thirst. He thought to himself if Ped' east was starting to suspect anything more. Kendall knew that he couldn't tell the pack about Jason in that respect, but he couldn't abandon the situation that he was in. He was enjoying himself. He gulped down the water from the fridge straight from the jug, something that his mother was always against. Kendall laughed at the thought as he put the jug on the counter, walked back to the living room floor, and finished his workout. Jason stepped out of the shower, still partially wet and wrapped in a towel.

"Hey Ken, you might want to get your funky behind into the shower if you are still going to the club," Jason said.

"Yeah, I am. I only have about five more minutes left in this workout. You know that I have to stay fine."

"You are already fine enough," Jason said. "But certainly not finer than me." He said, flexing his muscles in front of Kendall.

"Don't brag on yourself. You ain't all of that!" Kendall said, smiling.

"Please, are you trying to say that you don't think so?"

"Naw, you are fine. I'm just saying that you are not all of that."

"Okay then, that's what I wanted to hear. Now get your ass up and let's get rolling. It's later than you think."

Kendall put the weights down and rolled them over into the corner of the room where they usually sat, which gave his apartment that "bachelor look." He got up off of the floor and proceeded to walk past Jason. Jason popped him on the ass.

"Hey, don't start nothing you can't finish," Kendall said.

"Who said that I couldn't finish it?"

"Who said that I didn't want it to start?" Kendall raised his brow in devilment.

"Go get your musky ass in the shower, so that we can get out of here on time."

"I'm on my way." Kendall took off his sweat, drenched shirt on the way to the bathroom.

Kendall entered the bathroom and turned on the shower. He took off his clothes and got in. The semi-hot water that ran over his face and body seemed to loosen each of his tight muscles from his previous workout. Kendall had grabbed the soap and rag and lathered it good when Jason stepped into the shower.

"What are you doing here?"

"I just wanted some of that water to hit your musky body before I decided to start something that I can't finish," Jason said jokingly.

Jason took the soap and towel from Kendall and started up the lather again. He began to wash Kendall's chest and arms. He turned Kendall around and then started washing his back and buttocks. Kendall had no idea where this relationship was going, but the journey to wherever this place was had been great so far. As Jason stood behind him, Kendall could feel Jason's penis pressing against him. From behind, Jason took Kendall's penis into his hands and began to lather it up. Kendall thought that he was going insane. Both of them began to feel the heat, and it wasn't from the shower.

They would be a little late for the club tonight. There was already a performance going on.

The club was packed, and the line was wrapped around the building. Kendall and Jason walked past the line and up to the front door. Several people were mad because they could not get in and had been waiting for hours, and Kendall and Jason were about to get in after taking about thirty seconds to walk to the front door. Kendall gave the men at the door their names, and they were admitted into the club. On the way in, Kendall made a remark to the guy behind him that he knew would piss him off, "It is so good to have clout!" Kendall led Jason over to the club's usual spot, and there, Ped' east and D.J. were waiting. By the time Kendall reached the table, three ladies were leaving. Ped' east was giving autographs, with his new television show; he was the talk of the town. People enjoyed his show, and he had gathered a few groupies or loyal supports, as he called them.

"Hey, what's up, fellas?" Kendall said.

"What is up, my nigga" D.J. said. Kendall looked back at Jason with a sly inconspicuous smirk. That very phrase was the start of their relationship.

"What's happening?" Ped' east said. "Your ass is late."

"I know, I had some stuff to drop off at the post office on my way over here."

"Which post office did you use, the one in Canada?" Ped' east said sarcastically. Kendall flipped Ped' east his middle finger and turned to talk to D.J.

"Hey D.J., this is Jason. He works with me at the gym."

"What's up, man? How are you doing?" D.J. said, extending his hand.

"Fine. Thank you." Jason said back to him.

"Have a seat, fellas?" D.J. said.

"Where is Trip?" Kendall asked.

"I don't know, but I really need him to hurry his little ass up. I have things to do, and I need all of you here." D.J. said.

"What is the big fucking news already? I don't know why we have to do all of this waiting. Can you just go ahead and tell us?" Ped' east butted in.

"Chill out, playboy. It's not like you are going anywhere soon, and besides, I want to tell all of you as a group, and part of the group ain't here. Enjoy the music and the atmosphere." D.J. said.

D.J. reached for his cell phone to call Trip when he heard a loud scream from the door.

"Big brother, where you at? It's me, Trip, your little brother." Trip walked toward where the other brothers were. Trip walking strangely toward the men.

"Yo, big brother, what is up to, man? How you living?"

"Why are you talking so loud? What is wrong with you?" D.J. said.

"What do you mean? I feel great. Who the fuck is this?" Trip said, pointing to Jason.

"My name is Jason. How are you?" Jason said.

"Hey, I feel good," Trip said. "How about you, bruh?"

"I am also doing fine," Jason responded.

Trip sat down at the table with the rest of the pack.

"Hey, Jason, what is up, baby?" A beautiful woman walking past them stopped and said.

"Valencia, uhh, what's up, girl?" Jason slightly looked around.

He stood up and gave her a very welcoming hug.

"Nothing much, what are you doing here? I have never seen you here before."

"I know, I have never been here before."

"Come here for a second, and let me talk with you." She reached for him.

"A'ight. Hey, excuse me fellas. I will be right back."

Kendall's eyes followed them all the way to the other side of the nightclub. Jason excused himself without really waiting for a response. Kendall's wrinkled brow made Ped' east look strangely but didn't say anything. He probably would have said something, but Trip had started up again.

"Let's get it started!!!" Trip jumped up from the table, shouting.

"What is wrong with you? Why are you tripping?" D.J. said.

"Come on, man, you are embarrassing us!" Ped' east said.

"What the hell do y'all mean embarrassing you? This is a club, and you are supposed to be having a good time, so what am I doing wrong?" Trip said.

"Just sit down, Trip." D.J.'s voice seemed to rise.

"Who the hell are you yelling at?" Trip said.

"I'm not yelling at anyone. I am just asking you to sit down."

"You know, I am sick and tired of you always trying to tell me what to do. You are not my fucking parents. I don't know if you have noticed in the past five years that I am a grown-ass man, and I don't need your permission to do anything. Who the hell are you to try and chastise me, especially in this public place?" D.J. looked confused. He could not believe that his little brother was standing there, cussing him out in front of the people in the club. D.J. stood really close to Trip's face.

"What the hell is wrong with you? Why are you acting so strangely?"

"I'm not acting strangely. I am just me, and I don't have to apologize to your ass for who I am. Now excuse me, I have to piss, and I am going to the bathroom unless you would like to hold my hand and my dick for me, big brother!"

Trip walked off with pure anger in his eyes. D.J. slowly sat back down in the chair, and Ped' east touched his shoulder. Kendall was sitting at the table, but really was not at all concentrating on what was going on. All he could think about was Jason being gone for fifteen minutes without any sign or word of where he was and what he was doing.

"It's okay, man, you know how Trip is when he has gotten a little drink in his system." Ped' east said.

"Yeah, but I don't remember him drinking anything. Maybe he is really upset about something. Perhaps I need to go and check on him."

"Naw, man, just give him a minute to get himself together, and he will be fine."

"I know that I shouldn't, but I have to." D.J. got up from the table and started walking toward the bathroom where Trip went.

Kendall also got up from the table to see if he could find Jason. Ped' east was left at the table by himself. He signaled the waitress and asked her for a double shot of the strongest thing that they had. Kendall turned the corner of the club and walked right into a sight that he did not want to see. Jason was kissing the lady who he had left with. He turned around without being noticed and walked toward the bathroom. The surprise was too much for him. D.J. entered the bathroom but didn't see Trip. There were other people in the bathroom, so he didn't want to yell. He saw Trip's shirt through a crack in the bathroom stall. D.J. didn't see his pants pulled down to his ankles, so he figured that he was just sitting in the bathroom, trying to cool off from the argument that he had just had with him. D.J. walked to the stall and lightly opened it. As he opened it, he saw a small brown piece of paper with white powder sitting on Trip's lap. D.J. could saw the white residue of the powder on Trip's nose. D.J. could not believe his eyes.

"What the fuck are you doing?" D.J. said.

"Hey brother, it's not what you think."

"Have you lost your damn mind?" D.J. grabbed for the stuff, and Trip went to screaming.

"Leave my shit alone. Get the hell out of here."

"I can't believe that you are doing this." D.J.'s anger had come to ahead. D.J. grabbed Trip and pulled him out of the stall. The powder wasted to the floor.

"All my damn life, I have been taking care of your Lil' sorry ass. I cannot believe that you will do this to yourself and to me. I didn't think that your ass was that stupid."

"Fuck You!"

"Fuck me? Fuck me? Are you serious?" D.J. grabbed Trip and punched him in the face before he knew what had happened.

The two brothers began to fight in the bathroom. One guy ran out of the restroom, screaming, "Fight, fight, there is a fight in the bathroom, it's D.J." Kendall was already on his way to the bathroom, and Ped' east heard the news. He jumped across the VIP banister and ran to the bathroom. Kendall fought the crowd to get in, and so did Ped' east. Kendall tried to stop the fight, but he was pushed into the wall. D.J. was on top of Trip, punching him in the chest, face, and screaming at the top of his lungs.

"You ungrateful little bastard! How could you do this? How could you do this?"

"Come on, D.J., let him up, man. This is not cool. This is your brother." Kendall said.

Suddenly Ped' east broke through the crowd, and he and Kendall pulled D.J. off Trip. Trip was bloody and crying.

"You are my fucking brother, man. How could you do this to me? How could you embarrass me like this?" Trip said.

D.J. shook himself loose from Kendall and Ped' east. They were looking at him strangely. They were in agreement with Trip.

"What are y'all looking at? Why don't you ask Trip what the problem is? Why don't you let him tell you?" The fellas looked at Trip, but he didn't say anything.

"Cocaine, that's what. I found him in the bathroom, snorting Cocaine! Can you believe that?" D.J. said. Again, the fellas looked at Trip, but this time with a disappointed face.

"Come on nah, I know he is lying, Trip, isn't he?" Ped' east said.

"What is wrong with you, Trip?" Kendall said.

Trip got angry at the entire pack. "All of you can just stop looking at me like that. Just like I told D.J. I am a grown fucking man and whatever I want to do with my life, remember, it's my life. I don't need your pity, your concern, or your damn chastisement! Trip pushed through the guys surrounding them on his way out of the club.

"Trip, Trip, TRIP!" D.J. called, but he didn't answer.

"Don't worry, I'll go and get him and bring him home, and I will give you a call from there." Ped' east said.

"No man, I have to go and get him myself," D.J. said.

"Come on, man, he is not going to hear you right now. Let him go, and I can probably get through better than you at this moment. Listen, I promise, I will call you, trust me." Ped' east said.

"Man, that is my little brother," D.J. said.

"It's our little brother, too," Kendall said, "Let him handle it."

D.J. really didn't want them to, but he really saw no other choice. He knew that he couldn't sing tonight and that he had to go home. The crowd had disbursed, and D.J. went straight to the boss to tell him that he would not be singing tonight. Kendall was following D.J. when he saw Jason walking toward him. Kendall was already upset over what had just gone down with D.J. and Trip, and now Jason's presence would add fuel to the fire. Kendall thought that he would try to come to him with some explanation of what was going on with him and this girl, but actually, he was coming back to tell him that he would be leaving with her.

"What?" Kendall said with his voice barely a whisper.

"I am going to take a ride with Valencia. I will catch up with you later."

"What the hell is going on, Jason?"

"What do you mean?"

"I saw you and that girl kissing." Kendall was trying to contain himself, but he knew that he was getting emotional, which was not good. Lord knows he never thought in a million years that he would be talking to a guy with this much emotion.

"Come on, Kendall, you are tripping. We said that we would not do this. I will call you." Jason walked off and headed out of the door, leaving Kendall just standing there. Kendall felt his stomach starting to rumble. He reached into his pocket and pulled out some Tums. Meanwhile, D.J. was standing not far behind him. He didn't hear what they were saying, but he knew from the expression on Kendall's face and the way that Jason left, he knew that something was wrong.

"What is going on, Kendall?" D.J. said.

"Nothing, man, let's go."

This was one hell of a night, and it didn't seem that it would get any better.

CHAPTER THIRTEEN

D.J. tried his best to just give Trip some space before he would reach out to him, but he didn't have that much time. The news that he was trying to tell everyone was that he was going on tour with Zodana, and he was leaving shortly. He needed to talk with his brother.

He had been over there several times, but he got no answer. He kept in touch with Trip through Ped' east, but that was not much help because Trip didn't want to talk to him. It had been four days since the incident happened, and he had never gone that long without communicating with his brother, even when Trip was back home in Louisiana. D.J. didn't know what to do. He loved his brother dearly, and he didn't want leave on a wrong note. He and his brother had always been very close; this was the first real argument they had. D.J. flashed back on the first time that he had taken his little brother out to the movies and to "the levee." D.J. had just gotten his driver's license at age fifteen, and their parents did not believe in Halloween, so the boys could not go "trick or treating."

"Hey, D.J., thanks, man. That was a great movie."

"Hey, nothing is too good for my little man.

"Why come, daddy, 'em won't let us go trick or treating?"

"They just don't believe in it. Besides, do you have a problem hanging out with me?"

"Naw, I would rather be with you than anybody else."

D.J. could not take the pain that he was feeling.

He knew that Trip was at home, and he needed to get to him.

Although Trip didn't show it, he really needed his brother, D.J. thought. He was on his way over to Trip's crib. Maybe he would get through to him successfully.

Kendall sat on the couch, looking past the television. He was holding his stomach's comfort, a bottle of Pepto-Bismol. His stomach was killing him. At first, he thought that it was just his nerves that were giving him a weak stomach. He was about to worry himself silly about Jason. Kendall walked to the window to find that the rain had started its descent. His mind flashed back to the first time that they had made love, and the rain was pouring down. "How could I allow myself to get in this kind of mess? I don't know what to do." Kendall wanted to talk with his mother. It was times like these that nobody in the world could help you, but you could always depend on momma to kind of brighten your day. Kendall went to the phone and dialed the number. Maybe he would even have a small conversation with his father. That had not happened in a long while.

Kendall remembered back to the night when he found out that his football career was over. He was in so much pain, and he could not control the tears that ran down his face. His father never said anything, but he talked less and less and stayed away from more and more. Kendall hated what that meant as, in the past, he had always been so close to his father. Kendall was in a depression for months. He didn't know if he was in the depression because his football career was over or that his father knew he would never play football again; thus, he dreams of having a son in the NFL were gone.

"Hello."

"Hey, mom, how are you?"

"Kendall, is that you?"

"Yes, mother, it is me."

"How are you, baby. We have not heard from you in a while. I pray all the time for you. I miss you so much."

"I miss you too, mom. I don't want anything. I just haven't talked to y'all in a while, and I just wanted to see how everybody was doing."

"Well, chile, your Aunt Edna just bought a new car, and you know that she thinks that she is all of that. Fred, our neighbor, had kidney stones, and they had to rush him to the hospital the other day. Uh, that man was probably in a lot of pain. Oh, and ah Nancy's son, Tony, is back in prison again. Now you know that is a shame, and Betha's baby girl, done dropped out of college and is living with a man twice her age. What is this world coming too?" Kendall's mom chuckled to herself.

He knew that if he didn't stop her, she would go on forever. His mother loved to talk, and she always had the town's gossip.

"Mom, hey, I have to go."

"Oh, baby, I'm sorry. You don't call that often, and here I go talking about stuff that doesn't amount to a hill of beans."

"No, ma, it's not that. I just have some things to do."

"Okay, baby, momma loves you. You know that, don't you?"

"Yeah, I know."

"Hey, I also want you to know that your father loves you. I know that he is not the easiest person in the world to get along with, but he does."

"I know, talk to you later."

Kendall got off of the phone, not feeling any better than he had when he picked it up. Just then, the doorbell rang. Kendall ran to the door and opened it quickly without checking.

"Jason?"

"No, man, it's not Jason, it's me, D.J."

"Oh, what is up to, man?" Kendall seemed really disappointed.

"Damn, I'm sorry that I wasn't the one."

"Stop kidding around, man. What is up?"

D.J.'s happy expression changed. It seemed that he had reached an all-time low. He was not able to reach his brother. He had gone to see Trip, but he wasn't there.

"Ken, I can't find Trip, and I don't know what is going on with him. I know that he could not possibly still be mad."

"He's okay, he is just going through some hard times in his life. You know that we all go through that. You just have to give him a little space."

"Space? Didn't I tell you that Trip was snorting cocaine at the club? I have been by the studio and the agency, and he has not been to work. They are on the brink of firing him. Man, what if he loses his modeling gig?"

Kendall wanted to be into what was going on with D.J. and Trip, but he couldn't. The truth of the matter, he was having his own problems. He wanted to know where Jason was and why he had not called, come by, or said anything. It had been almost a week.

"Kendall, Kendall? You are not listening to me, man. What are you thinking about?"

"Nothing."

"You are lying."

"I'm not, man." Kendall was trying to hide his feelings, but he knew that D.J. saw straight through it.

"Man, you have been acting strangely for the longest."

"Nothing man, just leave it alone."

"Kendall, I have to be straight with you. Ped' east told me about some strange stuff that he has been seeing. Is there anything that you would like to tell me?"

"What are you talking about?"

"Come on, man, we have been friends all of our lives. If there is anything that you can't do is lie to me."

"Man, what are you talking about? What are you getting at?"

"Well, I am not the one to pass judgment on anything, and this is not about judgment, but I don't know how to react to this if you aren't straight with me."

"Be straight with you about what?" Kendall knew that he could hold off for long. Sooner or later, he would have to say something. He knew that he could trust D.J., but the conversation of him being in love with a man was too much for him to talk about. Kendall had never really considered himself being gay, nor had he ever used the word "love" in connection with Jason. For the first time in his life, he realized that he loved Jason, but he hadn't heard from him in almost a week.

"I want to know what is up with you and Jason. Ped' east said that he has been hearing and seeing some strange things. Things that usually would not happen between men." D.J. lifted his brow.

124

"Damn, Jay, why can't you just leave it alone? What do you want me to say? Do you want to hear that I have been in a relationship with a man? Do you want to hear that I have slept with a man? Do you want to hear that I am homosexual?" Kendall had finally said it. He admitted that he was gay. It felt good to his soul that he acknowledged it, but was afraid of the look that he would see on D.J.'s face.

"How come you never told me this? How long has this relationship been going on?"

"For about six months."

"Six months?"

"I know that I should have told you, but I was so ashamed about it. I am really finding out a lot of things about myself lately. Do you hate me, my brother?"

"First of all, don't be soft, you can be gay, but don't be a faggot." D.J. was trying to make Kendall laugh. And, he did, slightly.

"I ain't no faggot. I really don't know what I am. All I know is that I thought that I found someone who helped me to see the world better, and now Jason is nowhere to be found."

"How did all of this happen? Have you been feeling this way for a long time? What's the deal, man?"

Kendall knew that he was going to have to tell the story of Deacon's drama, as he called it, again. He never could say to this story without crying, but he wanted to be strong in front of his friend. D.J. could handle it, or so Kendall hoped. He started the long, mentally tiring story of how everything kicked off. Kendall felt the moisture welling up in his eyes, but he fought with everything that he had to keep them back. Halfway through the story, the doorbell rang. Kendall, in near tears, got up to answer the door. It was Jason.

"Well, I guess that I will be on my way. I bet you two have a lot to think about." D.J. said.

"Are you still my boy?"

"Come on, man, don't play with me. You know I love you, dude," D.J. gave Kendall a smile.

"Hey man, don't tell Ped' east what I told you, please."

"You know that you can count on me."

"One last thing, man," Kendall said.

"Yeah?"

"Don't give up on Trip. You know that he loves you. Find him and work this thing out."

"Yeah, I know, and I plan too." D.J. looked sad about the situation with his brother, but he seemed to understand what was going on with Kendall.

He didn't have the opportunity to really tell Kendall how he felt, but D.J. hoped for the chance to say to him that he loved him like a brother, and nothing would ever change that.

Kendall walked D.J. to the door as Jason moved out of the way to let them through. As Kendall shut the door, he took a long breath before turning around.

"I know that I have a lot of explaining to do."

"Hey, don't do me any favors."

"Listen. I have never been in the type of relationship that we have."

"And what type of relationship is that?" Kendall was trying to play dumb. He wanted Jason to know that he was mad, but he wasn't going to give him the satisfaction of seeing it firsthand.

"You are not gonna make this easy for me, are you?"

"Naw dog, that's not it. I want it to be easy for you. I want you to do what is best for you. Look, maybe we just made a big mistake. Perhaps we both needed to come to grips with knowing that this 'relationship' as you call it, just won't work."

"What is that supposed to mean?"

"It means that coming here a week later and wanting everything to be the way that it was is something that I don't tolerate. Never did and never will!" Kendall felt his father's spirit taking over him. He was going to get the last say.

"Kendall, I was deep into our relationship, and then I started to forget."

"Forget what?" Kendall felt his stomach boiling.

"Forget that I was in a relationship with a man."

"My bad brother, I thought that you knew I was a man." Kendall didn't want to show how pissed he was, but it was slowly but surely coming out.

126

"I didn't think of us as man and man. I just thought that you were the person who I loved."

Jason's spoken notion of loving Kendall made him stop in his tracks. He sat there, stunned by what he had just heard. He didn't know how to respond. His stomach was churning, and his heart was pacing fast.

"How can you love somebody and treat them the way that you did? I'm not some 'trick.' I know because I have hit them and left them too."

"You got it all wrong, Kendall. Something hit me at the club. When I saw Valencia, even though she was just an old girlfriend, at that exact moment, everything changed. It dawned on me that I was in love with you, and I wasn't sure that I wanted to live my life this way. I was with Val that night, but I was battling myself because all I could think about was you. Maybe I just needed to prove to myself if being with you was what I wanted to do, with no regrets and no shame."

"What do you mean being with me is what you wanted to do? Don't do me any favors?" Kendall seemed to be angry again.

"Being with you wasn't doing you a favor, but it was doing me a favor.

"I had sex with Val, but…"

"I don't want to hear this. Why don't you just leave the same way that you came in?" Kendall took a massive swig of the Pepto and headed for his room. Jason walked quickly behind him, grabbed his shoulders, and turned him around forcefully.

"Listen, please." Jason's voice died down. He loosened his grip on Kendall and began to speak in a calmer voice. "I did have sex with her, but I was thinking about you the whole time I was with her. I left her that night, knowing that my life was changing before my eyes, and it scared me. I know that you have not heard from me, but I had to clear my head. I needed to think things through. I know that it doesn't excuse what I did, but if it makes a difference for you to know, I want to spend the rest of my life with you. I love you, Kendall." Jason released Kendall, hoping to get a response.

Kendall didn't speak a word in response to what he had heard. All of what Jason had said totally shocked him. He was having the exact same feelings, but until tonight he had never verbalized them. Kendall knew he was still mad at Jason, but he loved him too, refusing to let him walk out of the door. Jason, in not hearing response at all, turned to walk toward the front door. With his eyes swelling with tears, he mustered up the words, "I love you, too!"

Jason turned around. He saw the tears stream down Kendall's face, and he understood them. Jason's eyes also began to tear. Neither of them saw those tears as a sign of weakness, but a common bond that would withstand time itself. The world around them seemed to stand silent, with only the beat of their hearts that guided one to the other like a weary ship being guided through the storm by the faithful lighthouse. Each tear rolled down Kendall's face was a healing process from all of the pains of the past; his relationship with his father, the ladies who seemed to vanish from his life without him ever finding true love, and the troubles that ate at his very existence. Jason was the core of his universe, his reason for holding on to this life when it seemed so appropriate for him to just let go. This would be the spirit that he would spend eternity with, and he knew that now. Kendall wanted to speak, but the reality of his connection to Jason took his breath away. Strong, affectionate, loving, and giving of himself were the characteristics of what made him love Jason, not his outer exterior, but his inner person.

They met each other in the middle of the hall. Jason wiped the tears from Kendall's eyes. His touch reassured him that any dark days in the future would be met head-on with a partner that not only would walk with him but also be his shield if that is what he needed. And, with a passionate kiss, he pledged himself to Kendall. Both of them could feel the energy they had between them. No matter what his upbringing spoke to him, no matter what the piercing stares of strangers and loved ones frowned upon him, this felt right, and whether the world in its traditional views approved, it just didn't matter. They had found what many others only dream of "true love."

Kendall led Jason to the bedroom. Although they had been there several times, this would be the first experience for them. Though this would be an uncharted journey, each was willing to let their destinies take them to wherever. As long as they would be together. What they shared between them could not possibly be defined with a societal label. They knew what it meant to love each other unconditionally. No words would be able to explain the emotions that would be displayed this night. Kendall, not in danger of losing his manhood, but finally feeling the healing of his inner pains, found peace and satisfaction in the arms of the person who was a perfect connection to his soul, Jason Dayries.

CHAPTER FOURTEEN

• • • • • • • ● • • • • • • •

Trip paced the living room floor. He lost his modeling job. Trip felt like his world was closing around him, and there was no one he could talk with. His drug urge was getting stronger, and he knew it, but there was nothing he could do about it. He picked up the phone a thousand times to call his brother but hung up before the second ring. He just couldn't do it. He knew his brother would ask him a lot of questions he wasn't ready to answer. Trip really didn't know what the hell was going on with life, but whatever cliff he had fallen off of, he was falling fast.

He sat on the floor next to the couch and thought about the dilemma he was in. He hated the fact that his only brother was not talking to him. Trip and his brother never argued, and the new distance between them was killing him. He wanted to speak with D.J. ever since they had fallen out in the club, but he just didn't know how. He was lost without his brother, and he was really feeling the absence of his presence. He knew D.J. was right and the only one he could ever confide in, but for a change, he wanted to show his big brother that he could take care of himself and knew he had messed everything up. Trip ran to the back room, where he kept his "nose candy." Tears began to fall from his eyes as he realized he now only had himself to depend on and the powder that lay before him. The family that he depended on was no longer there—mother, father, and now D.J.

Come on, man, pull yourself together. You are going to make it, and you are going to make everything better with D.J. Nothing can keep you down. You are a Cummings' man. Everything is going to be okay, everything is going to be fine, and everything is going to be okay.

Trip kept telling himself that, but the tears falling from his eyes made him realize that he was only fooling himself. D.J. would not forgive him for all the hell that he had put him through. The night in the club was the "straw that broke the camel's back." He had been the cause of many years of his brother's pain.

You stupid asshole! You are nothing but a waste. You really messed up any chance of having a normal life. Why is everything so complicated for you? Why can't you ever get anything right? Nobody is proud of you. You don't deserve love. Why don't you just kill yourself?

Trip tried to control the mixture of anger and disappointment welling up inside him, and no one wanted to help him. He had an angel on one shoulder and a demon on the other, but the demon's voice in his ear was winning. He felt like he deserved to die.

D.J. rode the freeway on his way to Trip's house. He had to get in touch with him. He had to make this thing right. Nothing in the world was worse than fighting with his brother. He knew that he shouldn't have hit him, but he was overwhelmed with the notion that Trip was on drugs, especially something like cocaine. He knew that those drugs would drag him down, and he had to make Trip see that. "Trip was finally getting his life together. Why would he allow himself to get caught up in a life like that?" D.J. wondered.

D.J. pulled off the freeway that led to Trip's house. He was determined this time to stay at the apartment until Trip showed up if he was not there. Trip's apartment complex was not far from the highway. As D.J. pulled into the apartment complex, he could see the light on from Trip's window, so he knew that Trip was home.

D.J. got out of the car very anxious to see his brother. This was a new feeling that he had not expected to have. It seemed as if he had not seen his brother in years, even though it had only been almost a week. As D.J. walked up the stairs to the inside of the building to catch the elevator, he knew that he would be leaving to go on tour with Zodana in the next three days, and he had to get things right with his brother. D.J. knocked on the door but got no answer. *"Come on, man, I know that you are in there. Please don't be this way. We are brothers."* D.J. thought to himself. He knocked again, but he heard no answer. Then he heard a thump, and the noise scared him. D.J. knocked on the door furiously. "Trip? Trip? Come on, man, open the door. Don't do this! Trip!" D.J. felt like something was wrong. He remembered that Trip kept a spare key in the dirt of the potted plant that sat a few inches away from the door. D.J. dug quickly through the soil of the plant to find the key. In haste, he found it. D.J. unlocked the door to find the safety chain on it. With a mighty kick, the latch went flying, and the door flung open. D.J. went into the house to find Trip lying on the floor, eyes closed, not breathing, and with blood pouring from his nose. There was powder all over his clothes and on the floor surrounding him.

"Trip? Trip? Oh, baby brother, what have you done?" D.J. ran to his brother, sat on the floor beside him, and pulled him into his lap. D.J. checked his brother's pulse and found that it was very faint. From the noise that he heard, he knew that his brother had not been lying there long. In total panic, D.J. ran to the phone and called 911.

"Hello, this is 911, can I help you?"

"Yes, my brother just overdosed. His pulse is faint, and he is unconscious. Please help!"

"Your name, please?"

"Dexton Cummings."

"What is the name of the injured?"

"Marcus Cummings."

"What seems to be the problem?"

"I just told you the damn problem! Can you get someone over here, now?"

"We have your address, sir, 112678 Phebus Street."

"Yes, that's it." D.J. was really upset.

"Is there an apartment number?"

"Yes, 217."

"Okay, sir, units have been dispatched now. Expect them in the next ten minutes. Do you know CPR?"

"Yes."

"Start it, and the paramedics will take over when they get there.

"Thank you," D.J. threw the phone down and ran back to his brother.

D.J. was shaking all over and crying heavily and screaming at Trip. *"Come on, Trip, don't you die on me, man. I need you, little brother. Daddy and mommy are gone, and I just cannot live without you. I love you, man, please come back to me, Trip. Don't you die on me, man!"*

D.J. held Trip tightly. The thought of losing his brother after losing his parents would be too much for him to take. He tore Trip's shirt open and started the CPR on him. "Where the fuck are the paramedics? What is taking them so long?" D.J. was angered at the ambulance, even though it had not been five minutes since the truck had been dispatched. D.J.'s tears seemed to cover Trip's face as he breathed into his mouth, trying to revive him. A mass of emotions seemed to go through him as he realized that he might lose his baby brother.

"Fight, Trip. Fight! I'm sorry that I wasn't there for you, little brother. Come on, Marcus, wake up. Come back to me." D.J. was tugging at Trip, trying to revive him. D.J. heard the ambulance. He knew that they would be there in just a few seconds. He wanted to wipe his eyes and try to gain his composure, but as he held on to his brother, he didn't care what anyone thought. The paramedics finally got to the scene, and D.J. stepped back as they tried to revive Trip. An I.V. was placed into his arm, and they had started CPR on him. D.J. struggled to the phone once again. He had to call the pack or at least one of them. He called Kendall first, but he got no answer, and so nervously, and with barely a straight voice, he left a message on his answering machine. He told Kendall to meet them at the hospital as soon as he could. D.J. then called Ped' east.

"Hello?"

"Ped' east, man," D.J.'s voice sounded like he was trembling.

"What is wrong, Jay?"

"Trip just overdosed. I am at his apartment now, and they are trying to revive him. I don't know if he is going to make it." D.J. started to cry again. He turned when he heard them say. His heart has stopped. Hook up the shockers. D.J. began screaming into the phone.

"His heart just stopped. Come on, Trip, man, fight!"

"Shit, don't panic man, I am coming right over."

"Okay, man, I'll see you when you get here, hurry!"

D.J. dropped the phone and went back to his brother. "Clear," the metallic shockers were again placed across Trip's chest. Trip's chest bucked from the power of the electricity that went through him. "My God, what if my brother dies, and I don't get the chance to fix this argument that we had and tell him that I love him." D.J. thought to himself. The paramedics shocked him once more, and his heartbeat returned, but faintly. D.J. sighed in relief, but he knew that his brother was not out of danger yet. The paramedics explained to him that they had to transport him to Community General Hospital. D.J. nodded in agreement and asked if he could ride in the ambulance. They agreed while placing Trip on the stretcher. D.J. was trying to lock the door when Ped' east came up the stairs. D.J. was a nervous wreck and couldn't seem to get it to lock. His knees began to buckle like he was going to faint himself. His eyes were burning from the tears.

"Damn, this stupid lock!" D.J. said.

"Calm down, man, I'll lock it. You go ahead with Trip. What hospital are you going to?"

"Community General" Ped' east hugged his friend as he saw the tears running down his face.

"It's gonna be alright, man, I promise you. Be strong."

D.J. ran down the stairs to leave with Trip. Getting in the ambulance and seeing his brother lying there was almost too much for him to handle. Just when he thought that he would be able to handle it, he started to cry again. D.J. sat in the spare seat close to his brother. He never saw his brother look like this before. He held his hand, hoping that Trip could feel that he was there and that he would always be there.

The ride to the hospital seems to take an eternity, but it gave D.J. time to think about what he needed to do. Even though Trip was a grown man, he could not leave him in this state. He knew that he would have to call Zodana and tell her that he couldn't go. He also knew that this would be the opportunity of a lifetime, but he could not afford to lose his brother. Trip means so much more to him than performing on a stage in front of people. Upon reaching the hospital, Trip was rushed to emergency surgery. It seemed that he had some internal bleeding also and damage to his brain and kidneys. The doctor found D.J. in the small hospital chapel. He went in to tell D.J. that the surgery could be unsuccessful, and even if he did come through the surgery, he might have some permanent damages. D.J. could not believe what he was hearing. The doctor left the room to get back to Trip. D.J. fell to his knees in the small, secluded area. He was grateful to be alone.

"Lord, I know that I don't talk with you often. I guess that I have been furious about the way that my parents left me." D.J. could barely speak. "I know that I am not supposed to question You for whatever reasons You do things that You do, but I am hurting so bad. My little brother means the world to me, and he is all that I have left. I know that You know that my brother and I got into a huge fight. I was amazed to see the youngster that I took a hand in raising was destroying himself. I am genuinely sorry for doing what I did to him. Lord, if I have to say goodbye, please allow me to tell him I'm sorry and love him. No, I want him back. I need him again. I would trade my own life in a heartbeat to save his. Maybe I am the wrong person to be even asking for any favors, but I beg You to please not take my brother."

D.J. felt as if his heart was melting. He felt like throwing something, but he knew that he had to control himself.

The walls of the room started to close on him. The tears were like an unattended faucet pouring from his face. Ped' east walked in.

"Don't do this to yourself, man."

"Ped' east, what if I lose him? What am I gonna do?" Ped' east hugged his friend. He wanted him to feel comfort. It felt just like the scene from couple of years ago when D.J. found out his parents had been killed.

"Trip is going to make it. What did the doctors say?"

"They don't know whether he is going to make it or not, and even if he does, he may not be the same Trip I know."

"There is a reason man that you are in this chapel. You have to believe that God is going to work everything out, alright."

Ped' east had never been a godly man, but spiritual encouragement seemed to be what D.J. needed, and it was what he felt in his heart to say. Even though Ped' east wanted to cry himself, he realized that he must be strong for D.J.

"Let's pray together. I'll say it," Ped' east said. Both of the men got on their knees at the tiny altar.

"Dear Lord, we come to You, first of all, thanking You for Your presence. We come on behalf of our brother. He needs You, Lord. We don't know what the outcome will be, but we ask that You give him a second chance. I pray for my brother D.J. that he can be strong during this troubling moment. Help us, for nothing can be done without You." Ped' east felt a hand on his shoulder. Kendall had gotten the message and arrived. *"Now we end this prayer thanking You for what You are already doing in the operating room. In Jesus' name. Amen."*

"Amen." The other two said in unison. Kendall hugged his brothers and tried his best to console D.J.

"All we can do now is wait," Kendall said.

"Everything is going to be fine. Trip is stubborn, and even if Death wanted to take him, he would give him hell, so Death would leave him alone." Ped' east said. Kendall gave a slight chuckle, and even D.J. had to admit. Trip was stubborn and pig-headed, so he smiled too.

"I just don't know what I would do without him," D.J. said.

"And you won't have to, homie." Ped' east said.

The fellas went into the waiting room to wait for the doctor's response to Trip's situation. As they walked in, Jason was in the place waiting for them. Ped' east looked strangely at D.J.

"How is he?" Jason asked.

"We still don't know. Trip's still in surgery," Kendall said.

"Did the doctor tell you anything before he went in?" Jason asked.

"Damn, would you like to go to the fucking operating room and have an interview?" Ped' east was pissed off at all of the questions.

"Excuse me?" Jason was at awe with Ped' east's response.

"What the hell are you doing here anyway?"

"Come on, Ped' east, you just gave a beautiful prayer in the chapel. How can you come in here and lose your cool like this? You have no reason to treat Jason that way." D.J. said.

"Besides, who put your ass in charge?" Kendall said.

"Oh, so I guess that he needs a bodyguard?" Ped' east said.

"How about I kick your fucking ass?!" Jason said. "Don't ever think that you can disrespect me." People in the waiting room started to stare.

"Come on, fellas, people are starting to stare," D.J. seemed furious. "My brother is in there fighting for his life, and you are all out here acting a fool."

"Jason was not backing down."" You know, it is bad enough that you don't know me at all! If I slammed your little ass in that fucking wall, you would give me more respect!"

"Come on then, you fucking faggot! What are you gonna do, throw a tampon at me?" Jason jumped at Ped' east; Kendall and D.J. got in between them. The nurse at the front desk called for security.

"What the hell is wrong with you, Ped' east? Have you lost your damn mind?" Kendall was furious.

"The question is, what is up with you, Kendall? What the hell is going on with you and him?" Ped' east had his mouth twisted in disgust.

"Who the hell do you think that you are passing judgment on me? We have been boys all of our lives! You have the nerve to stand there and talk to me like some nigga that a white policeman pinned against the wall.

"Fuck you, Ped' east! You and your bullshit is the reason that so much wrong shit happens in this world. I'll tell you who Jason is, not that I owe you a fucking explanation, but he is the person I love. So you can fix your face because I didn't ask for your damn approval." Kendall was furious. "D.J., call me when you hear from the doctors. I am going home. Come on, Jason."

By this time, no one in the waiting room had their attention someplace else. Everyone was focused on the "fight in waiting."

"Don't leave Kendall, please stay," D.J. said.

"Hey, I can't stay, but you know that I got your back." Kendall took one last look at Ped' east, who had gone speechless and walked out of the door. Jason was close behind.

"What the hell is your problem, man?" D.J. said to Ped' east.

"Look, I just wanted to know what was going on. It is just not right for two men to be together all of the time."

"I knew something was going on. Them, damn punks!"

"I cannot believe you. Who gives you the right to pass judgment? The beautiful thing about real friends is that their love is unconditional. We have been boys for all of our lives. How could you disrespect him in front of all of these people? It is not okay to disregard his feelings. You are out of order! I know that you found the girl of your dreams, but your shit wasn't on the up either. It is only now that things are starting to work out for you. Don't you sit and pass judgment like you are a damn angel, and anyway, Kendall has not done anything wrong. How can you be mad at him for being in love, even if you don't agree with who he is in love with? You are his brother, remember? Look, Trip needs all of us here, and now part of the pack is gone. You broke the code." D.J. thought about what he had just said to Ped' east. He had broken the code too. He felt the tears welling back into his eyes again. "What is happening to us? This is not the way that it was supposed to be. I thought that our lives would take off once we got to New York. It's not supposed to turn out like this. I can't fucking believe this shit!" D.J. sank into the comfort of the chair. He felt broken into pieces and didn't know how he could ever get fixed.

Ped' east stood motionlessly in the waiting room. He had not moved ever seen Kendall finished his last words and walked out of the hospital. He knew that he was out of order for his actions, but at the same time, he just couldn't come to grips with the reality of what Kendall had just told him. He had to leave. Trip's situation, Kendall's actions, and D.J.'s chastisement were too much for him to swallow at once. With no word of goodbye, he pulled out keys and walked out of the waiting room to go home or somewhere far away from the hospital.

Several hours had passed, and D.J. was still waiting. Kendall called D.J. on his cell phone, hoping that the situation would have changed, but he yet had not heard anything. D.J. got up from the chair to stretch his legs. They had started to go to sleep. He looked at his watch and realized that he had been in the hospital for six hours. D.J. knew that he needed to call Zodana. He couldn't go with her. He had no other dream in his life, but to be a singer but Marcus Cummings, III, meant much more to him than anything in this world. He refused to leave him, no matter what the sacrifice. D.J. took out his cell phone to call Zodana.

Ringgggg, ringgggg, ringgggggg

"Hello."

"Zodana?"

"Yeah, who is this?"

"It's me, D.J."

"Hey, Dexton, what's up? Are you getting ready to go?"

"Ah, that is the reason that I am calling you."

"What's wrong?" Zodana could hear the sadness in his voice.

"I had a terrible day."

"Hey, you are not telling me anything. I know that you have more to say than that. You can tell me. We are friends, aren't we?"

"Yeah, we are. I am at the hospital. My brother overdosed today. He's still alive so far, but he is in surgery."

"Are you serious? I'm sorry to hear that. Do you want me to come down there? Why didn't you call me earlier?"

"I didn't want to bother you. Besides, everything happened so fast I really didn't have a chance to do anything."

"Is there anything that I can do for you? Have you eaten?"

"No, I'm fine, but I do need to talk with you."

"You're not going, are you?"

D.J. paused for a second. "I can't go. I know that I am supposed to sign the papers tomorrow, but I can't leave my brother."

"D.J., I do understand, but I do want you to think about this. There are a lot of legal matters that got you to this point. You can't just give it up like that. Opportunities like this don't come around every day. I understand your problem, and in the same situation, I probably would do the same thing, but it's not that simple."

"It is that simple. I didn't sign any papers, and I am not leaving my brother. My parents are deceased, and I didn't even get a chance to say goodbye to either of them. I will be here for my brother!"

"I am not trying to be heartless, and if I am, please forgive me. I'll do my best to help you out in any way that I can. We're friends, right?"

"Of course, we are. Zodana, don't think that I am not appreciative because I am. I just can't leave Trip. He is all that I have in the world."

"I know, Dexton. I will talk with them tomorrow. See you around."

"See you, and good luck." D.J. hung up the phone and his career. He didn't care at this point. He wouldn't be able to concentrate miles away as his brother could be taking his last breath. He picked up his phone once again to give Aunt Kandy a call. He had to inform her of what was going on.

While he was talking to Aunt Kandy, one of the new resident doctors walked in, and D.J.'s heart dropped to the floor.

"Is there a Mr. Cummings present?" The young doctor asked.

"I am Mr. Cummings. How is my brother, doctor?"

"We repaired everything that we could. Your brother is out from the coma, and the damage to his liver was minor, but we can't seem to stop his internal bleeding on his brain." D.J. felt surrounded by a wall that seemed to be closing in on him every second. "What does that mean, doctor?"

"I'm sorry, he doesn't have much time left."

D.J. could not believe what he was hearing. D.J. dropped his phone as he heard Aunt Kandy scream in the background. After all of the prayers and worrying that he had done, nothing had worked. Tears instantly fell from his eyes as if they had been there all along.

"My brother is dying? Please tell me that is not what you are telling me."

"I'm sorry." the young doctor said, and with not that much experience in consoling, her eyes began to water. It would be a long road for her, in this career that often brought grief to a relative. D.J.

fell to his knees in agony. He was alone, and his brother was dying. He picked up the phone, and through tears, he told Aunt Kandy he would call her back.

With as much strength as he could muster, he asked, "Can I see him?"

"Sure, I'll take you there. Follow me."

The steps down the hall seemed to stretch forever. It was like walking the green mile. Every memory of his life with his brother flashed before his eyes. D.J. wished that he could get back the past five years of his life and did something different. Maybe he could have saved his parents, and perhaps if he had never come to New York, Trip might not have strayed into the path that he took. D.J. blamed himself for everything. He felt that he was the protector of his brother, and now he had let him fall to such an ill fate.

"Your brother is in this room. Don't talk with him long. He's tired and may not be that coherent."

"Thank you, doctor." D.J. wiped his eyes and tried to put on a smile. He knew that this was probably the hardest thing he would ever have to do. As he walked into the private room and saw all of the tubes connected to his brother, he could not help but cry. He quietly pulled the chair close to his brother's bed and took his brother's hand into his. The grabbing of Trip's hand awoke him.

"Hey, big brother. I have missed you." Trip voice sounded chalky and weary.

"Don't talk, Trip, save your strength." D.J. fought to hold back the tears, but he couldn't.

"Come on, man, it's alright. I'm gonna be fine. This life was boring anyway." Trip was trying to produce a slight smile.

"What am I gonna do without you?"

"You won't ever have to. I will always be with you."

"I am so sorry about our argument. I love you more than life itself. Please forgive me."

"Forgive you for what? You have always been the greatest thing in my life. I would never have made it this far without you. I am the one who is sorry for letting you down. All my life, all I ever wanted to do was to make you proud of me." Tears began to roll down Trip's face.

D.J. laid his head across Trip's chest. "I have always been proud of you." D.J. squeezed his hand tightly. He felt like he was choking. Trip reached up with his free hand and gently stroked the back of his big brother's neck.

"I need you to do me one last favor." Trip said, lifting D.J.'s head from the watery puddle he had made in his lap.

"What man, anything?"

"I need you to get the pack here. I want to spend my last bit of time left with all of you."

"Come on, man, stop talking like that. I'll find a doctor who can help you. You have to fight. If you give up…."

"D.J., D.J…Shhhhhh, I know the truth, and I did this to myself, and maybe this is the only way that I can have a better life, by starting over in another life." Trip started to cough. D.J. poured him a glass of water from the stand.

"I should have protected you. I know daddy and momma are turning over in their graves."

"This is not your fault. You could not have been a better brother, and I love you with all of my heart. Believe that!"

D.J. could actually hear his heart shattering. "Everything is going wrong. The fellas fell out earlier. They may never speak to each other again. I don't know if I will be able to get them here or not."

"Everything is going to be alright."

"I don't want to leave you for a minute."

"I don't ask you for much," Trip said jokingly, "Are you gonna get the fellas here or not?"

"Yeah, I'm on it." D.J. got up from the chair and lightly kissed his brother on the forehead and left out of the room.

"Hey, you know that I don't like all of that gay stuff." Trip offered a faint smile as best he could.

"You don't have a choice now, do you?" D.J. smiled back at him, I'll be back.

D.J. and Ped' east were at the front of the hospital waiting on Kendall. When they saw him drive up, Ped' east was glad to see that Jason was not in the car. Kendall parked as quickly as he could and ran straight to D.J. Totally ignoring Ped' east, he started asking questions.

"Is he alright? I got here as fast as I could." In Ped' east's rush to get there, he had the same questions but had not asked them. He was also anxious to know. The look on D.J.'s face let both of them know that something was wrong.

"Come on, man, say something!" Ped' east said.

"It's not looking good," D.J. said.

"What does that mean?" Kendall asked.

"Trip is dying."

"What?" Ped' east said seemingly in shock.

The fellas stood there for what seemed an eternity.

"We've got to get to him. Come on," Kendall said. D.J. led the fellas into the hospital and toward Trip's room. As they approached the room, Ped' east stopped. His eyes were filled with tears.

"I can't go in there, man. I don't want to see Trip like this."

"I know that it is hard, but he wanted me to get all of us together. Please be strong for him, and in fact, he doesn't need you to be. He's okay. Whatever reaction you have will be fine. We just need to be together for his last moments." Even though D.J. was teary-eyed, he had gotten strength from somewhere, but he couldn't explain where it was coming from. D.J. took Ped' east by the arm and gently led him into the room. Kendall followed behind.

Trip was looking out of the window, admiring the beautiful birds. He had a Bible lying across his lap. "I have been reading this Bible. It seems the most natural thing for me to do." Trip started talking before the guys could say anything. He really wanted them to hear him before they began to make any comments.

"I read in here," Trip gently patting the bible, "Where God watches over the smallest beasts of the land and the fowl in the air. It says that if he takes care of them, then surely, he will take care of me. I know that all of you think that I am not going to be okay, but I am. I have made my peace with God." Tears began to fall from the eyes of all of the pack, even Trip. "You three guys raised me, and I hope that something that I said or did will live with you forever. You never made me not feel a part of you, and for that, I am grateful. Each of you played an essential role in my life. You know, I thought that I came to New York to be famous, but now I know my purpose is to help you understand your purpose. I know that I am the youngest one, but for some reason, I see everything so clearly now. So please listen to me. Don't lose focus. It seems that in the rush of everyday life and our dreams of stardom, we forgot to live. I think that in the midst of it all, we are missing our blessings, waiting on a blessing. We are already successful! We have each other, and that is the way that it has always been. There are not many people who will ever have that. I love each of you! Forever and past time. Now come here."

The fellas could not contain the feelings that welled up from deep inside. Although saddened, they felt inspired. They slowly walked toward the bed, each hugging Trip in joyful tears. Ped' east and Kendall knew that friendship meant more than the price of gold and hugged each other.

"Big brother, come here." Trip's voice became fainter by every word. D.J. leaned down to Trip's face. "In this drawer over here, I have all of the things that I want for my funeral written down on a piece of paper. I promise to tell mom and dad you said hello. It's time." He kissed his brother. This was the first time that Trip openly and willingly showed affection to D.J., and he thought that time was standing still.

"No, Trip, Don't go, man!"

"It's okay. I'll be with you," Trip's voice was fading.

Kendall walked toward the bed and put up the cut finger of the pack in a final gesture. Ped' east knowing what he was doing joined in with his. D.J. looked up and added in his finger, and Trip, with the last ounce of strength he had, made the four complete. Within an instant, his finger fell, and Trip closed his beautiful green eyes for the last time and passed this life.

CHAPTER FIFTEEN

· · · · · · ● · · · · · · · ·

After all of the paperwork was done, Kendall drove D.J. to his house, and Ped' east followed. The fellas knew that D.J. was in no mood to drive home. Nothing was said on the ride to D.J.'s apartment. It seemed as if everyone was numb, almost in disbelief that Trip was really gone. D.J. seemed to be in a trance as his mind took him back through the words that Trip had said before his passing. He was so proud of how eloquently and strong his brother spoke. He thought his brother's courage; he knew he was dying but yet didn't fear what was to come. They were almost at the apartment complex, and D.J. started to fear the loneliness that he would encounter. He knew that Trip would never stop by the house, call, or even get on his nerves. With the loss of his parents, and now his only sibling, he felt disconnected from the world. He didn't have a steady girl, no children, and no family. Even though he had Kendall and Ped' east, it just didn't feel the same. Kendall parked the car, and Ped' east pulled in beside them. All of them went into the house. Ped' east tried to spark a conversation, but D.J. wasn't in the mood.

"D.J., I know that this is hard, but Trip would have wanted you to be alright." Ped' east said.

"Yeah, man, he is in a much better place now," Kendall said.

"We are going to get through this together," said Ped' east.

"You know that you won't have to go through this alone," Kendall said.

"Come on, man, say something," Ped' east motioned to D.J.

D.J.'s emotions started to change. He was no longer sad, but he was angry. He didn't understand what was going on. Everybody else's family was in tack, and his entire being had been disrupted.

145

"I don't fucking understand. I prayed, and I prayed, and you even prayed with me. I asked the Lord to please not take my brother. First, I had to lose my parents and now my ONLY brother. What have I done to deserve this? God owes me some answers, and I want them now." D.J. was screaming.

The fellas could see D.J.'s anger magnifying. They motioned to try to console him but decided to let him vent.

"Is this some sick payback that I have to accept for some sin that I committed? I do the best that I can, and this is the thanks that I get. My brother was too young to die. His life was just getting started!!" D.J. was screaming at the top of his lungs, "His life was not supposed to end like this. What the fuck is going on? My parents were upstanding citizens and role models for children as well as adults. I don't deserve this shit!" D.J. grabbed the end table and threw it against the wall.

"D.J., come on, man, calm down." Ped' east tried to grab for him, but he moved out the way. D.J. started to destroy things, his desk, pictures on the wall, and lamps in a rage. Kendall grabbed him and wrestled him to the floor. D.J. was crying hard.

"It's okay, man, it's okay," Kendall said.

"Why, Kendall? Why is this happening? Please tell me why this is happening."

"I don't know, man, but you're gonna make it."

"I'm not, man. I'm the only one left, and I want to go to. I want to die," D.J. could barely talk through his tears. "Just let me kill myself."

Ped' east didn't know what to say, so he sat on the floor beside the fellas and just hugged D.J.

"Listen, D.J.," Kendall said. "I know what it is like, man, wanting to die. I was there a few weeks ago. I felt like I couldn't tell anyone about my problems, and I just wanted to die. But, Jason was there, and he helped me through it. I made it, and now I know that I can go on." Kendall glanced at Ped' east from the corner of his eye when he spoke about Jason. "My point is there may be some dark days ahead, but sooner or later, the light has to show itself. And, for every dark day, me and Ped' east will be here."

D.J. continued to cry on Ped' east's shoulder.

"Go ahead, man, and get it all out." Ped' east was wiping tears from his own eyes, but he was still able to keep his composure strong enough for D.J.

"Come on, man, why don't you get some rest. You have been up for a while now, and I know you are exhausted. We are not going anywhere. When you wake up, we'll be here. Ain't that right, Ped' east?"

"You know it. Let's get you into bed."

Kendall and Ped' east helped D.J. get up off the floor.

It was almost dealing with some fragile child that had no concept of the world around him.

"I'll try to find him some aspirin to help him sleep while you get him out of those clothes." Ped' east said.

Kendall led D.J. down the hall to the bedroom. D.J.'s eyes were still moist, but he seemed to have stopped crying. Kendall pulled back the covers, and D.J. sat on the bed. Kendall took off his shoes and yanked off the warm gray sweats that he had on, and D.J. slid into the bed. Ped' east walked into the room with some aspirin and a cold glass of water. He put the pills in D.J.'s hands and handed him the glass of water. D.J. took them and lay back on the pillow. He was already out of it from the exhaustion. D.J. fell asleep instantly. Kendall turned off the light, and the fellas went back into the living room to straighten up.

After about thirty minutes, the room was back in order except for the broken items that could not be salvaged. They sat down on the couch, exhausted themselves.

"Kendall, man, I just wanted to say that I am sorry for all of the stupid stuff that I said and did to you. You know you, my boy?"

"It's okay. I am sorry too for all of the things that I said too."

"So, do you really love him?" Ped' east tried as best he could not to make negative facial expressions. He didn't want to get it started again.

"Yesterday morning, I would not be able to say this, but yeah, I do love him."

"Man, this is all so strange to me. Have y'all ever…you know?" Ped' east starting making gestures. Kendall started to smile.

"You're all in my business now. You don't ask people that."

"I guess that is my answer, huh?"

"Hey, I didn't say a word, but you can take it any way you like it." Kendall gave Ped' east a little more smile.

"Are you sure that you are gay?"

"From this point in my life, yeah, I am sure."

Ped' east wanted to understand, but he just didn't. He knew that Kendall meant a lot to him, but it would take some time to get used to Kendall being with another man, but he would do his best. For now, he just returned Kendall's smile. He even started to tell Kendall about Jessica and P.J.

All of a sudden, the boys heard D.J. screaming. They jumped up and ran into the room. D.J. was screaming in his sleep.

"Wake up, D.J.! Wake up, man!" Ped' east said. Kendall rushed in and started shaking him; D.J. woke up.

He was shaking and was sweating heavily.

"It's just a dream," Kendall said.

"Man, it seemed so real," D.J. said.

"What was the dream about?" Ped' east said.

"I dreamed that I was on the edge of a cliff, and Trip was falling, but I caught him right before he fell. The struggle was hard, but I promised him that I would not let him drop. At that moment, my hands started slipping. I started pulling with all of my might, and my parents were on the other side of the cliff shouting, "Don't let him fall, D.J." I started to pull harder, but the more I pulled, the more he slipped. I looked into his eyes, and he knew that he was going to fall, and he said to me, "It's okay; this is the only way that I will be able to stand on the other side with momma and pops." And then he slipped right out of my arms. I couldn't hold on. I couldn't hold on!"

"It's okay, Jay. It's just a dream, and you haven't lost him. None of us have. He will be with us in our hearts for the rest of our lives." The fellas hugged each other. All of them were in tears. This embrace made D.J. feel better. He, at that moment, understood the importance of the pack.

"Come on, man, you need to eat something," Kendall said.

"I'm not in the mood to eat," said D.J.

"You should always be in the mood to eat," Kendall said.

"Anyway, let's order a pizza. I'm hungry as hell." Ped' east said.

"I'm not hungry," D.J. said.

"Fine, but can you give me some money to buy it, and I'll eat your slices."

Ped' east was trying hard to get D.J. to lighten up. D.J. realized it and smiled at Ped' east.

"Alright, man, order the pizza. D.J. didn't feel hungry at all, but he knew that he couldn't sleep.

It took about an hour for the pizza to arrive, but the fellas filled in the time with happy memories of Trip, and they chased those memories with the *Jack Daniels* D.J. had in the cabinet. This hour would not be sad because Trip was the comedian of the group. Many memories of him goofing off, playing pranks, getting on everybody's nerves, all of the ugly girls who he dated that he thought were "off the hook," and especially, the way that he danced.

He was the best dancer from miles around. His little slim body could defy gravity. After the pizza and liquor were gone, the conversation of their memories of Trip, of each other, and growing up in Louisiana were still going strong. They finally fell asleep almost at daybreak.

Part Five:

Unchartered Territory

CHAPTER SIXTEEN

·········●●●●●●●●●●●●●●·····

D.J. received several offers to stay with relatives, but he really didn't want to deal with all of the questions about Trip. He decided to get a hotel until the funeral arrangements were done and finally lay his brother to rest beside his parents. As the airplane pulled into Baton Rouge Metro and the passengers started to deboard the plane, D.J., Kendall, and Ped' east knew that each of them would experience very different times back home. They all looked at each other and embraced the drama. They already knew that there would be some.

"Well, fellas, are y'all ready?" Kendall asked.

"About as ready as I am going to get," D.J. said.

"I'm ready for some of my mama's home cooking," Ped' east said.

"D.J., are you going to be alright?" Kendall said, starting to get up to deboard. The line was beginning to move.

"Yeah, I'm gonna be fine. I will be with my relatives, but I will come back to the comfort and quiet of the hotel room." D.J. said.

"Well, you know that we will be in touch with you every day?" Ped' east said. "Anything that you need, just call."

"I know, I only have three days to get this thing together, but I want it to be special. Trip deserved that much. I'll call you when I need you," D.J. said.

"Cool, cause I have some stuff that I want to throw at you a little later, D.J., but I don't want to tell you now. It might kill the surprise." Ped' east had a grin from ear to ear.

The fellas got off the plane and walked into the main terminal. Each of them was greeted by relatives. Ped' east's parents were there to pick him up; Kendall's older brother was there to pick him up; and

D.J.'s mother's sister, Aunt Kandiest, was there to pick him up. As the chatter resounded in the airport, each of them waved from afar.

"Hey, Aunt Kandy, how are you?"

"Oh, Lord, chile, how bad your sorrows must be." She gave him a big hug.

"I'm fine, Aunt Kandy, I'm just a little tired. I will be fine once I get to the hotel and get some sleep."

"Oh no, you don't! How you think you gon' come back to yo' home and sleep in a hotel? Your mother, God rest her soul, would kill me if and I do that! Besides, I know that your heart is aching, and I want to be there to help you mend it if you let me."

"But Auntie…"

"Naw, I don't want to hear another word about it. I'm an old widowed woman who doesn't take no for an answer. I don't get the chance to entertain anyone, and given the circumstances, you gon' need yo' Auntie, boy! I already cooked you a hot meal, and it's waiting for you at the house."

D.J. knew that he couldn't win. He was happy to feel the love from blood relations. Aunt Kandiest was his favorite aunt, and he guessed that it wouldn't be so bad. These next few days would be very hard on him.

Kendall walked into the house and sat his bag by the door. He took a deep breath as he followed his brother into the family room. The "pine-sol" from his mother's clean floors was a welcomed treat. The hallway led to the family room. It was the storage place for all of the trophies he and his brothers won throughout the years. His father built a trophy case for the hallway to hold all the awards the boys had received. Kendall stopped in front of the trophy case, and he knew that he was home. In the case was his first trophy, and beside it was a picture of him and his father holding up the award. Kendall was sitting in his father's lap, grinning from ear to ear. He walked to the room where his father was sitting in his chair watching the football game, as usual, and that would never change. He had been doing this same ritual since Kendall was a child.

"Hello, daddy," Kendall said.

"Hey."

"How are you doing?"

"Fine."

"Where is momma?"

"She went to the store to buy some pie crusts."

"So, what's new?"

"Nothing."

"Well, I gonna go ahead upstairs. I will talk with you later."

Kendall's father didn't respond. He just stared into the television. Kendall knew that nothing had changed. The same father who he left was the same one who he came back to. Kendall went upstairs to call Jason. He needed comfort.

D.J. finished off the checklist of everything that Trip wanted for his "home going" service. He had to make sure that everything was right. He felt that was the last honorable thing that he had to do for his little brother. He sent out all of the information, got in touch with all of his relatives and friends, acquired his old church "Greater New Galilee Baptist Church, and talked with his former pastor, Dr. Litt. The twist was that Trip did not want his services at the church, but at the Life Center, because it had a grand stage. Trip wanted an "Alvin Ailey" style funeral. He wanted to be placed at the bottom of the stage and wanted a few of his old dance members from his choreography days in Baton Rouge to dance a dedicatory piece for his funeral. Everything had to be perfect. People might think that it was strange, but D.J. didn't care. It was what Trip wanted.

It was about 9:30 that night, and D.J. was still thinking about Trip. He heard a knock and a sweet little voice say, "Dexton, baby, are you up? I hear you stirring?"

"Yes, Aunt Kandy, I'm up, come on in."

"Baby, you need to get some rest. I brought you some warm milk and cookies to help you sleep."

"I know, but I can't stop thinking about Trip. No matter how many days pass, it always seems like he is about to walk through that door. I am so miserable that I could die."

Aunt Kandy sat the tray with milk and cookies down on the dresser and sat on the bed beside D.J. and patted him on the leg. "Baby, you got to know that everything that happens is planned by God. I know how you feel. When I lost your uncle, I thought that I would not be able to make it. I don't have any children, and I felt that I would just waste away living in this big ole' house by myself. But you know, God has been good to me even in my heartache. Nobody but God got me through that time in my life, and it will be nobody but Him that will bring you through this. I promise you that, baby."

D.J. didn't know what to say. Tomorrow would definitely be the worst day of his life. Not only would he have to bury his brother, but he would be laying him to rest next to his parents.

"Get yourself some rest, baby. Tomorrow's a long day, but I will be there with you." Aunt Kandy smiled at him, kissed him on the forehead, and left the room.

About five minutes later, D.J.'s cell phone rang. It was Ped' east.

"I know that you probably are trying to go to sleep, but I told you that I had some important news to tell you."

"What is it, man?"

"Well, here goes. I got a recording deal for you. I took your demos to someone I know, and they listened to them, and they like you, and they want to sign you."

"What are you talking about?"

"Are you surprised, man?"

"Ped' east, I really appreciate what you are trying to do for me, but I can't sing anymore, I don't want to sing anymore. I don't have anything to sing about."

"Come on, man, I know that you are having some hard times, but what are you going to do the day after tomorrow and the days that follow that. Some people never get one opportunity that you had with Zodana, and you didn't take it, but now you are being given a second chance. That shit never happens in real life. Don't blow this."

"Look, man, I am sorry, but I don't want to talk about this. I only have a few hours before the funeral, and I have to get up early. I'll talk with you later."

Come on, D.J. I love you, my brother, and whatever you go through, I'm going through also. Don't think that I don't miss Trip, because if anyone does, I do. But I do know that Trip wants us to live, even if it just to keep his memory alive."

"You don't understand! You have everyone. I have no one."

"How can you say that? We may not have the same blood that runs through our veins, but we are brothers, and we always have been. Besides, we cut our fingers and mixed our blood years ago, and I thought it meant something. We have lived our lives by this creed that we have. Don't believe that you are in this by yourself, because you are not."

"Look, I have to go. I will talk with you later." D.J. hung up the phone confused and frustrated.

CHAPTER SEVENTEEN

Kendall woke up exceptionally early. He was catching his flight as soon as the funeral was over. Kendall stayed up most of the night, thinking about the conversation he wanted to have with his father. He didn't understand why his father was the way that he was. In some ways, he was just like him.

Kendall packed the last of his things. He knew Ped' east would be blowing for him pretty soon. Kendall had a great time with his mother and his brothers, but his father hadn't given him the time of day. He wanted his father to be proud of him, but it appeared that it would never happen. Taking it for what it was worth, he did enjoy sleeping in his old room, his mother's cooking, joking around with his brothers, and just the atmosphere of being home. Kendall picked up his bags and was walking to the door when he saw a letter on the stand. It was a letter from his father. Kendall could not believe it, and it kind of scared him. This was something that his father had never done before. What did it say inside? Kendall picked up the letter and sat down on the bed. He opened the letter and read it.

Dear Son,

This is a tough thing for me to do. I really don't know how to start. I have been your father all of your life, and it seems that for several years now, we have been strangers. I know that I am not the easiest person in the world to get along with. I do know that. You see, I have spent my life thinking that the world should be one way and just didn't dawn on me until you came home. When I looked into your face, I was missing one of the most important things in this world; you becoming the fine man that you are. I didn't know how to make it right. I didn't know where to start. It's funny, huh? A grown man not truly being able to express himself. I have worked for the plant for twenty-five years. I have had several men under my command that I give instructions to on a daily basis, and I can't communicate with my own son. This deeply bothers me, and I know that it does you.

I know that I don't talk much, and when I do, it probably isn't the best thing to say, but I do love you son, and I always have. I am proud of the way that you are taking care of yourself. You look good, and that was from no help from me. Please forgive me for not giving you the chance to have the father that you deserve.

I know that what is in this letter will not erase all of the hurt and pain that I have caused you, but I want to try. You help me to do better. I guess it is the only way a stubborn old fool like me will learn.

I don't know if this letter will help or make things worse, but I hope that we can start again. I need you, I miss you, and I love you. I really hope that you feel any of these sentiments for your old stubborn pops.

Dad.

Kendall raced down the stairs and into his father's arms. He hugged him tightly as if he had met his long, lost father for the first time. This was a great feeling to reunite with his father. Kendall had been waiting for this day for years.

"Son, I've been thinking about all of this for a long time. I'm old and set in my ways, but I know that I had to do something. When you came the other day, I wanted so badly to talk to you, but it was hard to face you knowing that you have made something of yourself without me."

"It's okay pop, I haven't actually reached out myself. I've been so afraid of disappointing you that I built up a wall that became too high for me to see over or able to climb. You think we can start again, father and son?"

"There is nothing that I want more! Today it finally came." The tears in both of their eyes showed the pain that melted away from the heat of love.

The Life Center was packed full of people. It was amazing to know that so many people remembered and loved Trip. This really made D.J. feel good. As D.J., Aunt Kandiest, the pack, and the rest of the family marched down the aisle to their seats, D.J. saw his brother sleeping peacefully in his white casket, trimmed in gold at the bottom of the stage. Trip was dressed in all white, and there seemed to be hundreds of flowers surrounding him. D.J. planned everything to a "tee." As the quiet music played on, the family took their seat, and the ceremony began. Several dance teams that Trip use to choreograph performed very spiritual numbers in dedication to him. It was a moment felt with calmness, respect, and admiration for Trip. The minister gave a very spiritual and uplifting eulogy. Everything was dignified and heartfelt.

As D.J. prepared to make the closing remarks, he took a deep breath and slowly walked to the podium. When D.J. walked past his brother's body, he felt peace. This was the first time since the entire thing happened that he felt this way. He made it to the stage and stood behind the podium.

"You cannot imagine how many times I have practiced what I am going to say up here, but I can only speak from my heart." D.J. looked down to see Kendall and Ped' east smiling at him. He was grateful for the support. "Marcus Cummings, III was my little brother. I did my very best to teach him everything that I knew about life and being a man. I thought that with my parents already in heaven, I would be the one to take care of him. Often, I never gave him credit for the man he already was without me. All of this time I thought that I was teaching him, but little did I know, he was actually teaching me. I learned how to love someone with my whole heart, and that being a man is much more than gender but dealing with responsibility. The most important lesson that he taught me was right before he died in the hospital; he said that so many people go through life, wishing for things that they already have. My brother taught me that love is the most significant thing that you can have, and even after the death of our parents, I have always been loved." D.J. looked directly at Kendall and Ped' east. He then looked up with tears in his eyes.

"Trip, wherever you are, I hope that you are listening. I love you, and I thank you for the lessons. I got it, Thank you." D.J. wiped his eyes. "I would like to close this service with a song that I want to dedicate to my little brother and to the two brothers that I have left, Kendall Johnson and Ped' east Jovan." D.J. took the mic from the stand and walked toward the middle of the stage. He motioned for the musicians to play. D.J. started to sing with more power and passion that he could have ever imagined.

I thought that life would be an easy road.
In time I found that pain was a heavy load.
I thought to rid myself of this tiresome road.
But all that glitters is not gold.
It took my brother and my friends to help me, and now I know that I can clearly see that love is the answer to all my problems today, for your friendship, love, and open heart has helped me guide my way......

At the end of the song, there was not a dry eye in the building. Those four little boys of yesterday, lying in the backyard dreaming of the great tomorrow, had finally found what they needed to know. What they had been looking for, they had all this time. LOVE.

Part Six:

ONE YEAR LATER

Chapter Eighteen

· · · · · · ●●● ● ●●●● · · · ·

"Dearly beloved, we are gathered here today in the sight of God and man to join together this couple in holy matrimony. Ped' east Antonio Jovan, do you take Jessica Elexandria Harvey to be your wife?

The ceremony was like that of a fairy tale. Ped' east, Jessica, and little Peddy were starting their life anew. In the sight of three hundred guests at Louisiana's State Capitol's rose garden, they gave themselves to each other.

Everyone from the minister to guests was asked to wear white. All of the shades of melanin contrasting uniquely under different styles of white dresses and suits; it was one of the most beautiful sights for miles.

At the reception, later on, that evening, Kendall gave the toast. "To my friend and brother, I wish you nothing but the best that life has to offer you. I know what it is like to experience true love, and that bond is stronger than anything that this life can bring your way." Kendall gave a slight, unnoticed look at Jason and then back to Ped' east, Jessica, and the audience. "I'll never forget all of the memories that we had growing up. It has taught me that everyone needs the company of family. I wish you, Jessica, and little Peddy nothing but love, happiness, and success. I love you, my brother." Everyone clapped, and there was not a dry eye in the place. "Last, but certainly not least, I would like you to hear this song dedicated to you by a new, but one of the greatest gospel recording artists of all time. My friend, your friend, and our brother, Mr. Dexton Jermaine Cummings." The music started, and D.J. walked out of the platform.

165

"I want to say that I am truly blessed to be here. God has been so good to me. During my storm, He has given me, you, Kendall, and you, Ped' east, nothing but the best, and we are so blessed. Ped' east and Jessica, I wish you nothing but the richest blessings of God. As I sing this song for you, my brother and my sister, I would like my fiancée Ms. Zodana Ryan to come out because without her by my side, I would be lost.

D.J. started to sing one of the most amazing songs. It was a dedication to God for being able to overcome obstacles with love.

To be continued.....

www.ingramcontent.com/pod-product-compliance
Lightning Source LLC
Chambersburg PA
CBHW051126260626
47170CB00005B/1686